Mang Yang Pass

A Vietnam Novel

JAMES VOELKER

CKBooks Publishing

No part of this book may be reproduced in any form or by any electronic or mechanical means, including information storage and retrieval systems, without permission in writing from the author, except by a reviewer who may quote brief passages in a review.

The Vietnam slang is nothing close to actual Vietnamese but only what Jim remembers they used and it is spelled phonetically.

The characters and events in this book are fictitious, though based on true events from Jim's time in Vietnam and from stories Jim collected from other Vietnam Vets.

Contact the author at https://aadwix.wixsite.com/jvoelkermangyangpass

Names: Voelker, James, author.
Title: Mang Yang Pass : a Vietnam novel / James Voelker.
Description: New Glarus, WI : CKBooks Publishing, 2023.
Identifiers: ISBN 978-1-949085-80-8 (paperback) | ISBN 978-1-949085-81-5 (ebook)
Subjects: LCSH: Vietnam War, 1961-1975--Fiction. | Vietnam--Fiction. | Historical fiction. | War stories. | Military fiction. | Action and adventure fiction. | BISAC: FICTION / War & Military. | FICTION / Historical / 20th Century / Post-World War II. | FICTION / Action & Adventure. | GSAFD: Historical fiction. | Adventure fiction. | War stories.
Classification: LCC PS3622.O35 M36 2023 (print) | LCC PS3622.O35 (ebook) | DDC 813/.6--dc23.
LCCN: 2023908573
All the images belong to James Voelker

Copyright © 2023 James Voelker
All Rights Reserved

CKBooks Publishing
PO Box 214
New Glarus, WI 53574
Ckbookspublishing.com

Billy,
this book is for you

CHAPTER 1

Possibly the third week of January, could have been the second week of February – I had lost track of time – we were scheduled for another supply run. It was 0500 and the platoon sergeants started putting all personnel on station for the day (also called a duty roster), which in layman's terms meant giving out work assignments. Sunrise was in one hour. We had a general idea of what our assignments were but the sergeants would confirm it. I was scheduled as the first watch in the gun box on the Iron Butterfly, one of six gun trucks that would protect the supply convoy to Cam Ranh Bay and the Navy supply base on the coast of the Pacific. This meant running the Mang Yang Pass, the road that ran along the Ia Drang Valley and the most dangerous stretch of road to the coast. Twice a week the 573's main duty was to supply all six units of the Central Highlands. Everything was shipped in. It meant putting your life on the line just as much as going out on patrol did.

It was time to form up, which meant stepping outside and standing in line along the boardwalk that ran in front of the mess hall. Each building in the camp had its own boardwalk in front of it. The boardwalk wasn't needed now but May through July, when it rained pretty much all day, it was the only way to get out of the mud. Step off the boardwalk and you stepped into five to six inches of mud. Some guys even walked around barefoot so they didn't have to keep cleaning their boots. Not much was done during the rainy season.

The Batmobile, the jeep that belonged to Captain Shorts and Sergeant Scheffler, rolled up to the mess hall of the 573. They parked and got out. The Batmobile was famous in the high country. The paint job told it all: a hand-painted insignia with a yellow background and black bat adorning the hood. It also had a whole new gun – a 60 caliber. Steve Hovel was the company artist. Everyone called him Shovel. The captain and Sergeant Scheffler were called Batman and Robin when they were on the radio.

First Sergeant Epler called us to attention, then called off the day's duty roster; we were a bunch of knuckle heads and so repeating what we had just been told by our platoon sergeants was not unusual. It was Epler's job to keep track of the 573's two hundred and fifty fully armed men's comings and goings, which took a hard hand. The company was spread thin, down from our normal three hundred to about two fifty and getting thinner, with five to six guys finishing their tours every week, so most of us had only four hours of sleep. That was normal, and that was all we were going to get. We needed twice as many men to control the roads, the back country, and mountaintops of this part of Nam. Most of this country belonged to Charlie – the Viet Cong – North Vietnam's savage guerilla fighters. It had been this way for a year; the Central Highlands were hundreds of miles of no man's land. We were losing control on the ground. We didn't want to lose that; the roads were our only way in and out. Our air power was the only thing that saved us.

Fifty men were just coming off night perimeter guard duty, the last troops to form up, then we were all here. They needed some sleep, which meant about three hours of shuteye. Some would be placed in the convoy as second gunners or second drivers. The supply run took us half a day because of the switchbacks, poor road conditions, and the enemy that was always waiting to take us out. For the first part of the day the night guards would be up in the gun box where they could sleep. Platoon or squad leaders put together a list of names for the day's patrol. No one wanted to go out on patrol, as usual. Short patrol meant walking the perimeter of the Highland bases, tearing apart NVA (North Vietnam Army) mortar pits, looking for signs of activity (campfires and trenches), filling in the trenches, or leaving Claymore mines.

First Sergeant Epler, the old man of the company at forty, was a gun-toting father figure. He had signed up for his second tour over here to try and see if he could help a friend out – a young Vietnamese boy. He was awarded the Bronze Star six months prior for something he did less than a mile from where he was standing now. He had over ten years in the 101st airborne and was an amateur boxer. He was also handy with a 45, which he always wore in a shoulder holster with a bandolier of ammunition. The first sergeant was a kindhearted hard nose.

When you signed into the company, which became your new home, you were assigned to a platoon and given directions to your living quarters, your hooch. A hooch was bulletproof, wrapped with half-inch steel sheets, surrounded by sandbags stacked up three feet high, sitting three feet from the hooch, with gun emplacements between the sandbags and the hooch. A hooch had no lights or water; it was lit by kerosene lamps or you used a flashlight. It held twenty to thirty guys, their cots with mosquito nets above them, and a few chairs. It got really smelly in the summer so we would sit on a bunker or in the perimeter trench, which was four feet deep and ran along the backside of all the hooches. Obviously, this trench was not used in the rainy season.

After you signed in, you were then asked about your qualifications with rifles, experience with mortars, artillery spotting, your driving skills, and if you knew how to count clicks. A click on an artillery piece equaled ten steps, which was how the artillery units knew where to drop the mortars. Whatever the Army trained you for was only the beginning. You were in now, and this was the front lines. Up here you lived by what you knew.

A squad leader would walk you down to your hooch, then someone from your platoon would walk you over to the armory to pick out a weapon of your choice. The armory (also called the dugout) was a twenty-yard long, above-ground bunker made of interlocking steel sheets normally used to create runways, the same sheets used on the hooches. Dirt was piled on the roof sheets, and sandbags were piled up along its sides, but unlike the hooches, the dugout had the added benefit of a venting system. It was a workshop for gunsmiths and a gathering place for off-duty soldiers, some of whom were interested in all types of weaponry, especially sniper rifles. It was where you went when you wanted to hang out. The tables, made of wooden boxes, ran the length of the armory. On both sides men slept in hammocks with two or three AM radios going, all set to the same station, because there was only one. For chairs we had old truck seats and benches that ran the length of the dugout and lighting from kerosene lanterns. Everyone was welcome, but you had to bring your own beer.

Just before you entered, the sign above the door read "Alice's Restaurant - Walk right in. Sit right down." This day we had two newbies, their first day on duty, and they were having their first look at the armory where they got to meet other men from the company. Replacements were hard to come by. They had come in hours ago by plane and caught a chopper ride over to the camp. The sky pilot dropped them and the mail on the CO's office roof, a one-light landing pad. About midnight First Sergeant Epler was waiting for them. He signed them into the company, and they handed over their 201 file – their military file. Epler would salute you, shake your hand, give you a walk-through of the camp and a small speech he gave every newbie who was in-country for the first time. It was his version of a welcome.

~ MANG YANG PASS ~

Epler was not very good with speeches, but he wanted you to know that he was the boss and his speech told you just that, with no maybes. "We don't have the time for stateside rituals. Hear my words, no medals for outstanding duties. No court-martial or article 15s. Do your duty or suffer the consequences, which is receive my right haymaker; I will shake hands with your face with a knuckle sandwich. A black eye from me is your first warning. If I can't trust you out of my sight, you will be my office assistant and my driver until your black eye goes away. If you're still out of line and in trouble, I'll make you look like a raccoon with two black eyes. All straight talk, no maybes, no BS."

He closed the little speech with the bad news: "If you're not running a convoy, you'll be going out on short patrols and scouting duty. Always leaving out one of the three corner gates through the wire, always on foot, at least three to four days, once around the airport." The airport was at the far end of the string of US bases in the high country. It started with Artillery Hill, just above us, then our camp – the 573, which was a supply station for food, cigarettes, alcohol, field gear, and other military products. We were also the bath processor – the place where the dead soldiers were taken and cleaned before they were shipped home. Then came the 173 Airborne camp, the fuel dump, Two Core – the South Vietnam Army camp and home to Special Forces – then the North Vietnam prison, and the 5th Marine Corps' camp, which was now pretty much empty, save for less than one hundred men. They were down from five hundred, which significantly curtailed our ability to do anything in the Highlands.

"Pack it and back it" meant long patrols, usually down the valley and over the border into Cambodia. It was only a two-day walk in good weather. That's with an eighty-pound pack, armed to the teeth, around and through bombed-out hillsides.

Napalm and agent orange drop-zone air strikes cannibalized entire hills with hit and missed vegetation and trees. The landscape looked somewhat like it had been in a forest fire with bomb craters. Other places the vegetation was so thick you couldn't see five feet in front of you. Not many helicopters rode when you were this far out.

Captain Shorts and First Sergeant Epler had finished breakfast and were looking for Billy in the mess hall. Walking over to his office, they ran into me and Sinkhoseitts – Sink for short – my roommate and hooch buddy. We were friends of Billy.

"Where's Billy?" the captain asked.

"We haven't seen him," I replied.

"Probably not up yet," Sink added. "It's early."

Billy was South Vietnamese and everybody's little brother. He got treated like family. Several GIs had taken an old Jeep out of the boneyard and rebuilt it for him. They lengthened all the floor petals so he was the only one that could drive it. He made some money by running his own little taxi service, a late-night, early-morning taxi to the brothel and the "Madame Butterflies," also referred to as "call girls" stateside, and a service to and from the officers' quarters – a very lucrative service. He was small in size but there was no age limit or license required for this old jeep.

Billy talked about wanting a small motorcycle to go off post. He grew up on this Army base camp and lived in a hooch with other soldiers. He had his own M-16. The 573 company's daily logbook showed he had lived on base longer than anyone else. He didn't remember his family or his village. He was brought on base about six years prior. A patrol found him in a small bombed-out village, ten clicks from Cambodia. Everyone knew they had to bring him back to base camp; they couldn't leave him. His wounds were open and infected, and he could not walk. The squad leader and other men took turns piggybacking him out. They think Billy was about eleven, possibly twelve years old. But no one knew. He was the sole survivor.

~ MANG YANG PASS ~

First Sergeant Epler put in the paperwork for adoption several times and wanted to bring him home. All the first sergeant could do now was put him to work. The Vietnam military was running short of soldiers so they wanted Billy too. Billy was very ambitious. He ran errands. He knew every corner of the twenty-acre camp and could find men who didn't want to be found. Sergeant Epler trained him to operate the field radio, which was kept in the CO's office. Billy enjoyed his work very much. He was always in contact with all the driver crews and the perimeter towers. We were his family. He lived and ate with us.

Being able to speak both languages, he also spent many hours monitoring other conversations from not only the South Vietnamese Army (SVA) but also the US posts. Captured Chinese telephones and Russian radios were kept in the dugout, and an almost-new Russian field radio was in the CO's office next to our field radios, also called squawk boxes. Some captured American radios were used by the North Vietnamese Army (NVA). They listened in to our conversations the same as we listened to them.

Billy could pick up North Vietnamese, sometimes even talking with them in their language. He knew many military terms, and even though they didn't know who he was, the North Vietnamese would talk business. He gave the Vietcong some information – a weather report, a road report – to gain their trust. Some of it was correct and some gave away their intentions and location. He talked the talk and walked the walk. He reported yesterday's many transmissions to the first sergeant, a lot coming from the north and boo koo from the Ho Chi Minh Trail. Some of it was in code. More than six field radios were chatting back and forth the last two days. Some from even farther out, coming in from the northwest. Some of the talk was foreign, possibly Chinese. Billy was not sure because of the very weak transmission. It seemed to be a mix, with more every day.

Three men walked over to the CO's Jeep and were going over which men to put out on point for the day. In a company this small, you knew everyone's good and bad habits. I remember a man who tried to get out of going on patrol saying he was bitten by a rat and wanted to go on sick call. The first sergeant said to "Go to hell. You're going out, you little coward."

Billy kept his own hours.

"I want to get his report," the captain said.

"Charlie's out there," Epler said, "Yesterday there were boo koo radio transmissions reported. There was shooting all night on three sides of the perimeter. They're looking for a way through our perimeter wire."

The 573 was situated on a hillside. Above us and across the road, in Artillery Hill, Chico, the first driver of the SS Alabama gun truck, had his crew fall together for the day's details. Two members of his crew, Tiny and Smoking Joe, were back from Rest and Recouperation (R&R). They decided the uniform for the day should be cut-off jungle fatigues with Hawaiian shirts.

Artillery Hill shot 105 or 175 howitzers for the units in the Highlands, throwing out mortars that could reach a couple miles out. You had to know the difference between incoming and outgoing round/shells. For incoming rounds you heard the shell whistle in and then an explosion and sometimes the ground would shake. For out-going rounds you heard the explosion then the whistle of the shell going over our heads. And if it was dark, you could see the shell changing color as it ran across the night sky. It was a pastime of ours to sit on the perimeter bunkers and watch the shelling at night.

Three gun trucks had been sent out of the 573 to wait for the convoy, and they parked on both sides of the road, the Iron Butterfly being one of them. I was on the Iron Butterfly with Steamer, Yogi, Doc Brian Murray, and Sam.

As Shorts and Epler went over the day's road trip, coming

out of the darkness, two old gun trucks slowly and quietly drove up. Side-by-side, the crews harassed each other, back and forth, talking trash about their families and giving coyote howls – it was time to roll. They lined up at the front gate waiting; this was what these young soldiers lived for. It was an all-volunteer crew because we were told the life expectancy on a gun truck was four months. But not many people gave up this job, anxious for the chance to run the pass and to be a crew member on the green elephants – the name we gave military vehicles on a road trip. It was dangerous work, but it meant riding instead of walking. And with the rainy season lasting from June to November, a chance to stay out of the mud was not something easily passed up. It would keep our adrenaline moving for hours on end. Keep our hearts pumping, strong enough to move our uniform and flak jacket, all before sunup.

The two well-seasoned gun truck crews revved their engines, lined up right behind the Batmobile; they were the CO's bodyguard. The first gun truck, Ground Pounder, had a five-man crew. Today Tom McNulty was the first driver, Flunky was the second driver and a sharpshooter (he filled in when McNulty needed a rest or was busy doing other things), and Sink was one of the sharpshooters, like me. All of the guys who rode on the gun trucks would switch around between the trucks. Ground Pounder had the longest running record, with many years of running the Mang Yang Pass.

The other truck, Instant Hell, was a war wagon – it had a lot of potential. It had more 50-caliber guns than all the other gun trucks, and the crewmen were nineteen years old or younger but still a well-seasoned crew. Lefty was the driver, and Bogard was the radio man.

Captain Shorts walked over with First Sergeant Epler. As the captain talked with Scheffler, Epler gave Shorts information about the number of trucks and road conditions to the supply harbor at

~ JAMES VOELKER ~

Cam Ranh Bay. Merchant Marines brought in the supplies and the 573rd picked them up for all the units in the Highlands, though most of the soldiers in Nam were based along the ocean. We also might drop stuff off from past runs on our way down: fuel or food or alcohol; there was always alcohol.

Road maps and Epler's intel would help the CO figure out what roads were in the best shape. Epler wanted to add some merchandise to Sergeant Scheffler's shopping list, just a small list of material: two air conditioners for the office and one air-conditioner for his girlfriend. With a smile on his face, he added a case of booze; anything would be welcome, even tequila would work.

They finished their business with some small talk, then looked over all three vehicles. All was ready. Time to "de de mow," which meant "get up and go" in Vietnamese. A three-legged dog, the company mascot, a five-year-old German shepherd, walked over to the Batmobile and jumped in. He'd been given a new name; he was now called Tripod. He nosed around in the rear seat, eating whatever he could find. Both trainer and Tripod lost a leg while out on morning patrol, doing point and scouting duty. One of them stepped on a land mine. Both were airlifted out and given good recovery treatment. The dog came back. The man was shipped home.

Sergeant Scheffler called, "Tripod."

Tripod lifted his head up and showed them his teeth, then moved to the center of the rear seat; he was not done nosing around.

"Out! No ride today," Scheffler commanded.

Tripod nodded his head yes but wouldn't get out. Tripod was waiting for orders for his trip home to the states; his wounds all healed. He lived in the CO's office and slept under a table in the mess hall. Everyone looked after him.

The first sergeant stood in front of the jeep and stared at

~ MANG YANG PASS ~

Tripod, eye to eye. "This is an order. Stand down. No ride today. Inside, pronto!"

Scheffler talked to everybody in that same tone of voice.

Tripod jumped out and slowly walked over to the mess hall. Soldiers coming and going left the door open for him. He walked around the tables, enjoying table scraps.

Jumping into the jeep, Batman and Robin, with their gun-truck bodyguard, moved out. Doing a U-turn, they drove back 500 yards to the horseshoe driveway and a line of trucks waiting for the word to move out of the motor pool. Captain Shorts picked up the microphone on the field radio then gave the word.

"Do the road."

Everyone repeated the order: "Time to do the road!"

The front gate and road were calling our names.

Instant Hell was the second gun truck following the Batmobile. Radio calls began flowing. Over two dozen trucks waited in the predawn darkness: 18-wheelers, flatbed trucks, most of them empty and ready to be filled up, some with junk ready to trade or sell. In the gun box of Instant Hell, Bogard was on the squawk box talking with Lefty, the driver, who was already powering up, keeping close to the Batmobile, which was still in a lower gear. They moved around the motor pool horseshoe driveway, Ground Pounder right behind them. Lefty slammed up one gear for speed. He had to keep his right hand on the shifter; the transmission was so old and loose it wanted to pop out of gear. They ran less than a half minute behind the CO's jeep. All the radio men were shouting and requesting permission to de de mow.

A half dozen of the 18-wheeler crewmen were still loading up. Bogard was standing up on the corner wall of the gun box of Instant Hell, which was reinforced half-inch steel. He gave the coyote howl and the hand signal, rolling his hands in front of him – the basketball signal for traveling. The first set of flatbeds began moving out, some still waiting for their crews to assemble. They had run back into their hooches for their weapons or cigarettes. Hooches were the second line of defense and were fifty yards in from the main perimeter. The main first defense perimeter was a five-foot berm with bunkers every thirty feet, which had steel-plated sides walls with many pock marks and grease off incoming rounds. Past the berm were corner gun towers and concertina wire ringed by a multitude of explosive Claymore mines.

Pushing the old vehicles for everything they had, no driver yielded the right of way. Big Ray LaValley drove a flatbed loaded down with four old 175-artillery barrels and other scrap iron made up of two old helicopters, all roped down with old concertina wire. The old speed demon, LaValley, increased speed, going up two gears, then going on the squawk box shouting, "Hammer down!"

Flunky was on the field radio to the other three assembly points outside the camp. They were waiting and watching for the signal to roll. Flunky got his nickname working for his father's horse farm in Santa Barbara. He was a hard-core biker who got into too much trouble. A judge gave him a choice of going to jail or going into the Army. He had a perfect personality for this kind of work.

All the gun-truck crews were shouting back and forth over the noise. It was still total darkness. The only lights you could see were from the mess hall.

McNulty got on the radio to his good friend topside, Flunky, telling him to put up the colors with a flashlight.

"Put out the call to the other assembly points. Time to roll."

Flunky was talking to over twenty green elephant trucks. He went on the headset, trying to talk to a crew member.

He pointed to Sink, then to his headphones, wanting Sink to put his headphones on so he could talk to him. It was something you had to do with the noise of the trucks and in the darkness. He told Sink and the flatbeds and tankers, "We're on the move. Everyone hold on!" They were headed for the first turn.

The radio small talk got louder as everyone called out their place in the convoy.

Captain Shorts put out another call; time to "Do the road."

The field radios came alive again. The last of the men climbed on. Some ran, just making it. Bogard gave the signal to another group of flatbeds, then a wolf call. Running almost side-by-side the trucks moved out of the motor pool. In the gun trucks the guys were holding onto their guns in the gun box, which was in the back of a gun truck. They were shouting to each other, raising their right hand, moving it up and down, giving the power signal. Behind them a small spot of morning light appeared; the day was beginning. The 573 green elephants moved out, speeding up and spreading out.

Chico started up the SS Alabama, which was waiting outside the gate. The SS Alabama was a solid-frame, five-ton truck, twice the size of the other gun trucks and had been fully converted over into a flagship gun truck. All the other gun trucks were only two-and-a-half-ton military supply vehicles. All the gun trucks had ten wheels: two in front, eight in back. The SS Alabama had been totally rebuilt several times and customized again with side-by-side gun stands in the gun box, made with rollers capable of making a 360-degree turn. Most parts were borrowed from the Air Force. It was maintained and run completely with personnel from the 3rd Battalion, some of them from Alabama. None of them white. They were a very tough and proud bunch of outlaws, all from Artillery Hill.

These vehicles had been built from the experience of many trips up and down Mang Yang Pass, which wasn't anything more than a jeep trail. Stateside, these vehicles would be junk, overdue for scrap iron, too old, with worn-out tires, missing and loose bolts, and bullet holes. All from runs up and down Mang Yang Pass. The trucks had all been rebuilt many times from the boneyard. Customized to be bullet proof, all the glass had been replaced with half-inch steel. All the four-foot sidewalls of the gun box were recycled steel. The bottom of the gun box floor was covered with ammo boxes you had to walk on.

For speed a second gas tank filled with JP4 jet fuel, which we called nitro, was kept topside, behind the driver. We became self-taught scientists, coming up with an ingenious way to increase power by adding a second gas line, "a gravity flow turbocharger," which we only used while the vehicle was running. The nitro JP4 gave the vehicle almost twice the power of normal diesel fuel. The topside group did the mixing, when called for by the driver.

Chico was on the truck radio doing the duty roster checklist with his radioman and top gun.

"Get ready. How's the gas? Is the ammo dry? Check the breach."

Everyone was ready. They gave hand signals and shouted to Richard, trying to get his attention, shouting loud obscenities to the second driver, Smoking Joe. Chico wanted Richard to put on his headphones.

Smoking Joe was a Southside Chicago resident. He had actually signed up to follow in his father's footsteps. Everyone jokingly called him Smoking Joe. Most people didn't know his real name. He was well over six foot, and his arm muscles looked like tree stumps. He stood topside, right behind Chico, who was in the driver's seat right below him. This gun truck was a battleship with reinforced decking, a 105 howitzer on the center post in the gun box, two 106 howitzer artillery pieces, and four other machine guns.

The SS Alabama was always the last vehicle, the rear guard, so they couldn't always see what was coming up. They might move ahead but would always circle back.

"I want everything loaded and ready," Chico yelled into his headset.

A slight glow of sunlight was beginning to show itself. As usual, the two lead gun trucks were moving toward a muddy pond of mess hall wastewater. It was a mosquito-infested smelly mudhole from the kitchen's brown, soupy mud with some green food particles floating around the edges. Batman and Robin made a sharp right turn, not going through the stinky runoff. Aiming right for the center of the mudhole, Ground Pounder took the lead in front and to the inside of the convoy, rear wheels sending up a rooster tail of garbage and muddy water the length of the vehicle. Losing traction, McNulty straightened the steering wheel, shifted down one gear, then powered up again. Small, orange flames were seen coming out of the smokestack.

Instant Hell was one hundred feet behind, playing catch-up for lead, first one out the front gate, lead gun truck for the day. Over-steering, almost as if on an icy road, Lefty glided Instant Hell through the center of the pea-soup pond. Not letting off the gas pedal, he lost control, hydroplaning over the water without turning the steering wheel and ending up facing the opposite direction.

Lefty called out, "Damn truck. You sorry sack of shit."

"Give me more nitro!" he called up to Bogard.

Lefty downshifted and poured on the power. The rear wheels were sinking down into the bubbling water.

Bogard and the rest of the crew looked over the side, then he slowly dumped in a half gallon of JP4. At the same time Lefty let go of the clutch, coming out of the hole as the rear wheels sent a brown wastewater rooster-tail of mud and sewage water all over the mess doors and walls, hitting the foot traffic on the board walk. Troopers coming for breakfast scattered; some ran back inside, and more ran around the corner. They knew the routine by this time. Instant Hell still had not caught up to Ground Pounder.

Night guard security police (SPs for short) moved the concertina wire, which opened up to the road, then they all quickly jumped behind the reinforced sandbags to avoid getting hit. The second assembly point came up quickly, only a half mile out by Artillery Hill.

Batman and Robin were straight ahead. Captain Shorts was searching behind his seat, moving military hardware, a half-empty ammo box, some loaded weapons, a field gear ammo belt with a 45 handgun, and hand grenades. After every pothole the old Jeep bounced through, the storage area became all the worse. Captain Shorts moved handfuls of 60-caliber bandoliers, searching farther back in the storage area behind the seats, looking for his flare gun. The captain started to get an attitude.

"Damn it, Scheffler. It's your duty to clean the Batmobile. Get Epler on the horn. I want to know when Billy comes in."

"It's always my turn. When is it your turn? You make me do all the driving!"

Captain Shorts, who hadn't shaved in a week, gave a not-so-serious smile then with his right hand pointed to the two bars on his dirty uniform and then pointed to the convoy behind them. The freight train on wheels was leaving. The radio was alive with complaining, swearing, and name-calling.

Instant Hell had come up behind Ground Pounder and started playing bumper tag.

Big Ray called in. "I'm overloaded. I'm gonna hang back."

Lefty still wasn't done complaining.

"What motherfucker gave that asshole a driver's license?"

Three or four of the drivers immediately responded, saying they didn't know you needed a driver's license; you just had to be crazy enough to want this job.

The freight train was picking up speed as the last vehicles were coming out of the 573. For another hour more military vehicles would be joining the freight train. For the next five miles we moved at full speed.

Captain Shorts quit searching around and sat back down in the passenger seat. He found his flare gun. It was right behind his seat. He started swearing at Scheffler.

"That's not where I put it, God damn it!"

Scheffler replied, "Yes, it is."

Shorts immediately brought down his eyebrows and gave him an order. "Shut up and drive."

With that the captain fired his flare gun. The 573, the last outpost and supply base for the Highlands, was on the move.

The roads in Nam were totally uncontrolled, so it was the job of the gun trucks to get the vehicles back and forth from the coast with their loads. Muddy clay flew off the tires and mixed with the brown and reddish dust. Some low spots were still holding the morning fog, just enough to look like smoke. Visibility was bad that morning. You couldn't hear much over the sound of the truck motors, but you could see the leaves and branches moving in the wind as the trucks moved along the road. None of the crew had ear plugs so most of the GIs kept their headphones on. Everyone else used cigarette filters for ear protection.

Sunrise was slowly beginning. Orange, red, and streaks of yellow filled the sky. You could almost smell the heat. The sky was clear, and the last stars were blinking off.

The men knew to be ready. Captain Shorts was receiving his call from camp. Billy was reporting boo koo radio talk that morning. Special Forces and Montagnard troops – Montagnard villagers that had been given guns, fought alongside us and did some scouting for us – hadn't reported in yet. They had asked for more ammo and were requesting resupply by chopper at first daylight. More transmissions were coming in from farther out, from the north and the hilltops, twice the number as three days ago. That meant trouble.

CHAPTER 2

Captain Shorts signed off, "Over and out." Then he put out a call to the convoy. "Everyone keep your eyes open on the hilltops."

He pulled the rain poncho off their 60 caliber and gave it a looking over. Then he checked their ammo supply and put the poncho back over the weapon to keep the dust off. Captain Norman Shorts looked like an enlisted man in his dirty, old uniform, his normally fairly light skin weather beaten, with a baked-in suntan. His driver, Sergeant Scheffler – the company clerk – was called "Five Fingers." He signed orders and, after hours, ran the trading post. He was well connected. On payday he had been known to sell individual soldiers higher ranks for a small fee, no questions asked. As a black-market supplier, he made everything legal on paper and oversaw illegal midnight supplying for a profit. He was a good person to know in the Central Highlands. You couldn't wait for paperwork to supply your field units.

Captain Shorts, today's pathfinder (the person who called out directions), Ground Pounder, and Instant Hell all slowed, moving past Artillery Hill. Waiting in the morning shadows, was a line of flatbeds just off the road, watching for the SS Alabama with its green "Everything a go" flag and the word to "Do the road."

Two more gun trucks reported for duty over the radio: Iron Butterfly and Big Daddy Vergo Rat. The 573 got Iron Butterfly from Fort Wade Davis, the Marine Corps' unit in the Highlands.

"Out of the way. We're fueled up and ready to roll," was the transmission from Iron Butterfly.

The caller was Doc Murray. He had a field hospital in the mountains where he patched up the locals. He was talking with Captain Shorts about a special supply he heard about. He wanted to add five or six hard-to-find medical items to Sergeant Scheffler's list. He couldn't ask the Army for what he needed because the Montagnard people of the Highlands, a very primitive culture, who hunted with spears and crossbows made from old military parts, weren't in the Army, but they were on our side. They were looked down upon by other locals because of their dark skin and were usually treated poorly by them.

Captain Shorts was looking at Scheffler and nodding his head yes. With a tone of concern in his voice, he told Doc Murray, "I'm always willing to help a friend. We'll talk when we get to Mamasan's bakery. I'm sure we can work out a deal."

Doc wanted to come along on the needed supply grab. Whiskey Train was the fifth gun truck from the 573. They moved out with a half dozen empty tankers. Coming alongside Iron Butterfly, Whiskey Train's driver, Burnie, wanted to start the day with a race. These two gun trucks powered up and were trying to get past Instant Hell. The three gun trucks were running side-by-side, taking up the entire road and for just a moment were name-calling and saluting each other with one finger.

Off the radio Shorts and Scheffler had a high-pitched conversation about the shopping list. We all called it "market research," which meant Search Out and Steal (SOS).

The 173rd Airborne was a mile down and across the road from Artillery Hill. Waiting there were eight empty 18-wheelers. As always, the 18-wheelers wanted the entire world to know they were there, that they were running the road, so they shouted and whistled into the walkie-talkies.

Big Daddy Virgo Rat was one of the worst gun trucks as far

as having a big mouth. The crew chief and driver, Ammatwozeo, and his good friend and radioman, Rocky, called in and gave orders, wanting everyone to move over. At the same time Rocky fired off his flare gun, letting everyone know they were coming out. Behind him all the rest of the flatbeds did the same. The CO counted fifteen flares. Rocky got on the horn and called in his duty roster, moving past the SS Alabama. They were signaling each other with a flashlight. The flashlights had a red filter and were used to get someone's attention, to get their part of the road.

Rocky shouted out, "Coming through!"

He wanted more road. Ammatwozeo had to bring the vehicle halfway off the road to keep up speed. Giving a wolf call, Rocky fired off a second flare. These two guys invented road rage and driving under the influence, and as always were the loudest brainstorming road warriors in the convoy, always brainstorming alternative plans.

Rocky came on the radio, shouting at the top of his lungs. "This is Big Daddy calling in!" With a few four-letter words he added, "Get out of the way, motherfuckers. Eat my dust, move over, and give me some road!" Then he started singing some country western song about driving and his girlfriend. The convoy drivers didn't have many rules since you couldn't lose your driver's license. Besides, most of the guys didn't have a license anyway.

Six gun trucks were running that day. Cowboy, on Big Daddy, called me on the radio. I was ten vehicles in front of them on Iron Butterfly. Corpsman Doc Murray and I were talking over the road trip. It was a long run down to the ocean, but we wanted to hear some details.

Captain Shorts called back. He wanted a report and a radio call with Billy and then with First Sergeant Epler.

Minutes later Two Core headquarters called, giving Shorts some new information to pass onto Sergeant O'Riley. O'Riley was already in the convoy.

"Make sure O'Riley gets everything he needs. I want a bodyguard on him and his crew. You have to make sure he doesn't get arrested."

Captain Shorts looked over to his driver and nodded yes. Then, still listening to more of the conversation with this first sergeant at Two Core, Captain Shorts looked back at Scheffler and shook his head no, then signed off and set down the radio's microphone.

"I know you have things going with O'Riley," said Shorts. "He's not the person you think. That old Irishman is a black-market kingpin. To start with he's not a sergeant; he gets orders from Washington DC. His Special Forces and South Korean friends don't take any lip service. O'Riley takes orders from God and everyone else farther up the command chain, but he wants people to think of him as a good old sergeant."

Scheffler looked at the captain with a smile and added, "I've got a lot of money on tonight's extra curriculars. This is a big deal."

"O'Riley has a lot of new people for this outing," Shorts said. "The last seven days they've put together quite the shopping list."

Five-finger Scheffler pushed his helmet back and with a straight face turned and looked at the captain. "Some of that's mine. I've got a deal worked out with that whole crew. It's my job tonight to keep the shore patrol busy while the night crew does business in the Air Force and Navy yard supply bases. I've already sold two medium-sized generators."

Then Scheffler smiled and pulled out a notebook from the side pocket of his jungle fatigues, waving it in the air. "This is the South Korean Army shopping list too. They keep adding more materials."

"O'Riley may not even be in the Army, so we can't touch him. His orders came from Saigon headquarters, direct from DC. He worked with battalion headquarters – Two Core. He's got his fingers into many high command places at the South Vietnamese headquarters at Two Core. People see him walking around in civilian clothes with government officials. He goes to the airport and disappears for weeks. My orders are to aid and protect him, babysit his behind, get him back to Two Core headquarters, no questions asked."

Chapter 3

On the road now the convoy was moving along and heading down country, off the last plateau of the high country. Daylight was just beginning; we could just barely see the road. Sergeant Scheffler was driving along and eating a can of C-rations, not hard to do traveling thirty miles per hour. With a mouthful of food he went over the plans for the day with the captain. To prove his point, he waved the spoon in the air and pointed it at the captain, then with a big grin scooped up another mouthful of cold, gourmet stomach bomb.

Shorts watched him and replied, "I can't believe you just ate breakfast and you're hungry again. When that comes out of you, I don't want to be around."

Batman and Robin were on their third tour and had made friends and enemies. The North Vietnamese Army had actually placed bounties on their heads, which made them feel bigger than life. The two of them were from the same city on the East Coast, back in the world.

Captain Shorts dug under some ammo boxes to find another flare for his gun. "That's not where I put it last week. It should be right behind my seat!"

He pulled out a flare, loaded one round, and fired it straight up — the signal for time to speed up. The Batmobile was a fully armed command post on wheels. The front bumper had a reinforced

~ MANG YANG PASS ~

S-shaped wire cutter coming up and over the hood almost to the windshield, where it bent forward, a sharp edge in the bend for cutting wire. The Vietcong would string wire across the road to take off your head.

The vehicle had a collection of necessities, with everything just thrown in the back seat. The collection included rain ponchos and some half-eaten C-ration cans. A loaded and ready 60 caliber was wrapped up in an old rain poncho and mounted on a center post just behind the windshield, loaded with 5000 rounds. Two M79 grenade launchers (like a sawed-off shot gun) were hanging right behind the driver's seat, where either man could reach over and pull it out of its case with one hand.

The captain was famous for his road trips. He actually turned down an appointed office job in Washington DC to stay in country for his family's name. Like his men, he was good in the field. He wouldn't order someone to do something he wouldn't do himself. He almost got court-martialed a couple of times for doing just that, which had earned him respect when we were on the road and over time.

All his troops respected him. In Vietnam that was a hard thing to make happen. More than half the men under his command were nineteen years old. Some lied about their age and signed up at seventeen, not wanting to miss the chance to go to war. These young men all came for the opportunity and glory, to honor and to serve. When still in their street clothes, called zero week, they raised their right hand and pledged to God and country to obey all orders from their commanders. Then altogether saluted the flag, with no hesitation, taking one step forward and standing at attention, doing "eyes right" toward the flag. But about half the guys didn't want to be there. They'd hide from details or get put on KP (kitchen patrol). They liked being on the convoys verses going out on patrol.

Everyone went by a nickname out here. To get a good one

you had to keep up, blend in, and be willing to keep the outpost running, for the grand total of five tax-free dollars a day and two cans of cold and old C-rations. The C-rations didn't have expiration dates. Everybody called C-rations C-rats; some were left over from WWII or the Korean War, which meant we were eating a meal that was older than the soldier. Many of the men would eat Vietnamese food, which was monkey meat with rice or hotdogs and was made from real dog. If you could catch one, snakes were very good, if they were fried just right, but you had to be careful about the Bamboo Viper. If you killed one, you had to cut the head off. Still better than Army chow.

CHAPTER 4

The sun was breaking through the horizon. With it came the Asian heat. Captain Shorts, on the field radio to his gun truck bodyguard radioman, Sink, told him to send up a flashlight with the yellow flag, the caution sign. It was still too early to see the flags in the morning darkness but we could see the flag with a working flashlight wired to the top of the antenna. Instant Hell saw the signal, pulled down their whip antenna, and attached a flashlight and an American flag with the yellow flag. The call went out, "Everyone send up a flashlight with the yellow flag."

We slowed down but didn't stop at the next assembly point, the base camp called Sandbag Point. There, nine more flatbeds were waiting with two reefer trucks (refrigerator trucks), ready to roll down Highway QL 14.

Steamer, the driver of Iron Butterfly, radioed the convoy, "Everyone, make eligible room; I'm moving up!" Steamer roamed around, moving up to the front, three or four miles, doing a U-turn, and going back to see Chico, who was always at the rear.

The long line of vehicles moved to the right side. Steamer was a road master, a self-proclaimed crew chief.

Ammatwozeo, on Big Daddy Virgo Rat, got on the horn, calling in a welcome to the last vehicles to the convoy. "Welcome, assholes. I hope you're ready to die. We're all ready to rock and roll."

Ammatwozeo was from Hoboken, New Jersey, and he had

a very heavy Jersey accent. He put out a call telling everyone to "Put the hammer down and speed up!"

Ground Pounder and Iron Butterfly were still calling each other four-letter words and insulting each other's body parts. Showing the quality of his upbringing, Jerry Jeff Whitelaw called Lefty and me.

"Listen to those assholes. Together their IQ isn't even double digits."

I couldn't let that go, of course. "Jerry Jeff is so ugly his mother must've been a man."

Sink shouted, "What did you say?"

Jerry Jeff replied, "Your mom's a guy!"

Big Ray, Ray LaValley, broke into the radio conversation and called out to Jerry Jeff, "Throw JV off the side. I'll run over his head. That big mouth, rat fink is cruisin' for a brusin'."

LaValley had a different reason for being there. He volunteered for the Army after high school to look for his lost brother, Edward, who went missing in action in the high country three years ago. His last letter home said he was up here for three months doing recon. LaValley was on a personal mission, so he spent time communicating with the Army and his brother's old company, looking for answers.

LaValley got on the radio. "Everyone, knock off the racket!"

Sink cut in. "Get your helmet on; some bad bush is coming up. Lock and load. If you're looking for a war, you're in the right place at the right time for a firefight."

Captain Shorts broke in, telling everyone to quiet down.

Ammatwozeo got in the last word. "Put it where the sun don't shine, LaValley."

Then Captain Shorts came on the radio for the second time. "All gun trucks and rifleman, keep your eyes open on the hilltops. Things are about to get hot."

Shovel, the second driver with LaValley, added, "I don't want any bullet holes in my new paint job!"

Big Daddy Virgo Rat had a handcrafted paint job designed by Shovel and Yogi, in the California style of Ed Roth, displayed on the doors and hood. It featured a rat cartoon character standing upright with an ugly beer belly in bright blue overalls. The writing below the rat in black letters was a quote of Roth's: "You have the right of way halfway under this vehicle." It was signed "ER."

Yogi came on the squawk box reporting for duty. Another familiar voice was heard over the radio. An old friend of mine, Cowboy, gave a call going out to all crew chiefs.

"Time to bring down the antenna and send up two flashlights and a green flag." Time to put on some miles.

Shotgun Eddie on the Whiskey Train replied, "It's already been done. Do the road!"

Cowboy came back with a wolf howl. "I'm short. I'm a two-digit midget with only ninety-eight days left!" He ended with another wolf howl.

Being short, or a short-timer, meant you had less than one hundred days left in country. Anyone who was short counted down the days.

Born in the small town of Eaton, Colorado, Cowboy was a member of the Ute Indian tribe. He was the radioman and sometimes the driver, but when things got busy with incoming rounds, he picked up the 60 caliber. Cowboy had been around rifles since he was a child, when he went on family hunting trips into the Rocky Mountains. He earned his name in his tribal tradition and was given an eagle feather, which he kept on his helmet. He told everybody it gave him strength and control over his spirit. You become a citizen and a member of the Indian nation of the Ute when you become a hunter. He didn't brag about his rifle skills and didn't talk about anything else, either. His father was a full-blooded Ute Indian and rancher. The two of them went to Denver, and his dad signed the enlistment papers for his son at seventeen, telling him there would be many more hunts in the Rockies when he came home a veteran.

Another call came in. It was Captain Shorts, trying to get our attention. The radio was still alive with conversations. The radio system kept our minds off the many miles of road ahead. It would take us all day to get to the port.

Coming over a small hill and a slow right turn, the Batmobile almost ran into an old three-wheeled Lambretta scooter in the morning shadows. Three South Vietnamese farmers were hauling a live boar pig easily weighing over 300 pounds. They had it in a bamboo cage in the back of the Lambretta and the three men squeezed into the front seat. The Vietnamese didn't have cattle or sheep because they didn't have anything to feed them. Pigs ate anything. Captain Shorts came within a foot of the back corner of the cage and the pig's wet nose. The old vehicle was barely visible in the darkness.

Scheffler moved up alongside, then shouted and signaled them to move off the road. They nodded their heads yes, then waved back, enjoying their loosely rolled cigarettes. The three-wheeled motorcycle barely moved, almost bouncing down the center of the highway.

It was the only transportation these farmers had, most likely the only vehicle the family had. This was their livelihood. The men were the counterweights to hold down the old scooter. Transporting this dirty boar pig was a challenge. The three-wheeler was rocking down the road. The three Vietnamese were holding onto the vehicle with a disconcerting straight-ahead look. They were moving too slow, trying to control a huge animal, which was their most valuable possession for trading with other farmers.

The Batmobile didn't have time to be courteous. This very old and over-used Lambretta was in harm's way and was going to be roadkill in minutes. This vehicle had to go; it had to be moved off the road.

The farmers waved goodbye, still not getting the idea.

Captain Shorts shouted one more time and pointed to the side of the road, then the captain ran his finger across his neck and shouted out twice, "Oona wanna die? Second warning. You must pull off!"

The driver and his friends just shook their heads and smiled, cigarette in hand. The captain could hear something like "Wooua, wooua," meaning yes in their native tongue.

The captain had to move this vehicle off the road since they were only a few minutes behind a freight train of vehicles, and they were coming up to several large turns in the road, which required the trucks to hold tight to the hillside and rock formations.

It would all be downhill, after that. That's when all hell started. Captain Shorts was on the field radio to Sink and Flunky in Ground Pounder, talking over the first problem of the day. This small vehicle had to be pushed aside.

When the lead gun truck came out of the darkness and dust, all three of the Vietnamese looked at the vehicle behind them. The gun truck didn't have its lights on, no one did; only one small taillight was used to keep track of the rear light section on each truck, but the Vietnamese could hear the engine only five feet away bearing down, coming in closer. The farmers and the pig saw small flames coming out from both smokestacks. The driver, McNulty, was on his field radio with the CO.

"You gotta push them off the road, McNulty, slowly."

The gun truck inched up, closing behind the three-wheeled animal taxi. Bumper-to-bumper. At this point the captain had moved to the rear of the Jeep, standing up to get a better view of the old Lambretta. He was on the walkie-talkie, signaling the distance between the two vehicles behind him.

The Vietnamese farmers were starting to realize the problem.

Sink, up in the cargo bay, stood right behind the driver. McNulty was talking to Sink on the truck's communication system.

Captain Shorts called out, "Do the snowplow and hurry up!"

With that McNulty began to push forward. Sink tapped him on the helmet – also called a steel pot – when the time was right. Ground Pounder's front bumpers were padded and reinforced with old tires. The truck moved forward, connecting his bumper to the very small vehicle on the far right corner, careful not to run over the personnel but to run the vehicle off the road. The push started raising the rear half of the motor scooter. You could see the three Vietnamese farmers had realized their problem.

Sink gave the order to increase the speed for five seconds. Then he backed off. Again he came up and pushed a little harder and backed off again. Even the pig was watching and trying to get away, kicking his back legs, his four-inch tusks rattling his bamboo container. The Vietnamese were complaining and shouting. You could hear some four-letter words: "Duo Mammie. Muck Yii!"

Finally off the road, the farmers and their pig would live and continue on in an hour or more. McNulty was enjoying the job. He had a degree in journalism before coming into the Army. Every week Tom mailed home a column of newspaper copy of their encounters in the Central Highlands, which was published in his local paper.

He signaled to the radioman to send out the word; the road was clear. The Batmobile sped up and went back out on point.

CHAPTER 5

*I*nstant Hell was on the field radio to Batman and Robin. "Freight train coming up fast, only minutes behind." They were moving up the line.

A dust storm from the trucks almost looked like smoke. There was just barely enough morning light to see. The convoy drivers avoided the dust by traveling only ten or fewer feet apart. The sunrise was on the hilltops but it was still dark on the road. As they traveled alongside the edge of the cliffs, the morning light moved down the hillside of the vast Ia Drang Valley. For hundreds of miles or more, the next three or four hours was all a downgrade.

On his field radio, the CO wanted air support and put out a call. "Put some snakes in the air." Meaning time for the Cobra helicopter gunships to lift off. He knew what was coming on the road ahead, and we needed air backup.

The freight train had already gone past the point of no return. The CO fired another flare straight up, which gave the gunships a direction to head for, to "do the road" from the air. Six gun trucks and more than twenty tankers were moving down the road with ten or more flatbeds loaded with broken-down helicopters and old trucks stripped down to the bone. Some carried old howitzer barrels forty feet long, eight inches in diameter, worn out from sending hundreds of rounds into Bullet Hole Woods, otherwise known as Cambodia. Add to that a dozen or more refrigerated units running the road. These vehicles were everybody's meal ticket.

Bad roads and steep hills made convoy trucks a very easy target. Coming up on the first bridge over one of the many small rivers guarded by the Korean Rock Army, Captain Shorts put up another flare. All the vehicles slowed down, shifting to their lower gears. He called out on the radio the names of drivers to pull off and offload, then he asked Big Daddy Virgo Rat to drop off for security. This was called a "Stop and Go," a quick re-supply. Then they played catch-up to the rest of the convoy, rejoining the convoy on Highway 14 going south, continuing down country.

The Koreans guarded the bridges. They were mercenaries paid by the American government to keep the bridges open. Five trucks in all dropped off supplies with one gun truck bodyguard. Then it was back on the road.

All the crews were back on the radio again. They were all talking and giving orders but not listening to anyone. Another fast stop for a small base camp called LZ Snowy Mountain, right next

~ MANG YANG PASS ~

to Chu Se, a small village. Captain Shorts called certain vehicles to come off the road and do another drop off at LZ Snowy Mountain, a fire base for about thirty Special Forces soldiers with a couple howitzers. There were a few of these bases – 100 x 100 foot square with 105 or 175 howitzer artillery. If the base was called a Rose Garden, it meant they could land a helicopter inside the base. This firebase was one of the many in the Central Highlands and was a listening post where they sent people out a mile or two to listen to where the enemy was. The Army troops from Snowy Mountain were on the roadside, waiting to flag us down to drop off their supplies.

Three flatbeds with fuel, artillery shells, and other military essentials were dropped off with a refrigerated supply truck. They only delivered essentials today. They dropped off fully loaded trailers and hooked up to empty flatbed trailers.

Snowy Mountain was a hilltop firebase. Built in one hour by some sky pilots who simply dropped a handful of 500-pounders, blowing the top off a heavily forested hill. And when the dust cleared, they called the bomb crater a firebase camp. But they had a small problem; two 500-pound bombs didn't detonate; they were still live. They bounced off a couple of trees and came in for a soft landing. They were leaning on their sides and didn't explode. The demolition team wouldn't blow them in place. They had placed Claymore anti-personnel explosives behind each one and would use them for defense if and when it was needed. The Montagnard people had been warned not to hammer on or try and disassemble them, which they might have tried to do. Montagnard people were just learning the modern ways of war.

As we left the Ia Drang Valley, the next camp we came upon was another hilltop base, a Special Forces outpost called Nhon Hoa, also called the Elephant Village. This was base camp for the 11th Light Cavalry Special Forces. They had four 105 artillery pieces. Special Forces were specially trained men who had usually been in the service for five to six years. Here the Special Forces were joined by an entire village of Montagnard soldiers and families, who mobilized only when needed from miles around. They were the best scouts in the High Country. They lead the Special Forces, most of the times living in their small huts along the fields. They raised their animals and crops along the higher cliffs among the irrigated fields. Many had a new crop introduced by the Americans: corn. They were raising corn for their animals and had rice paddies, which they had cultivated for hundreds of years. The Montagnard people were very primitive. They made their own clothes and used spears and crossbows to hunt. And if they were captured by the NVA, they were treated with contempt and used as slaves, forced labor to carry supplies and weapons and used to dig. Montagnard troops didn't care for uniforms. They only wore their native clothing with a shirt. Their boots were on order for smaller sizes, along with an order for smaller stockings.

The hilltop camp had two Huey UH 1 cargo helicopters, one on each side of the front gate. The helicopters were so badly shot up, coming in hot – under fire – they were unable to lift off and were now being used like guard towers.

Bases out here were close enough to reinforce each other. We were dropping off their supplies and picking up a half dozen men who were going down country for one reason or another.

Captain Shorts came on the field radio again, calling out names of the drivers for the next drop-off. He also called Ammatwozero on Big Daddy Virgo Rat. He wanted them to drop off for security again. The convoy drivers had a thirty-minute layover for this Stop and Go. It was the same MO (modus operandi): dropping off full trailers, then switching and picking up empty ones before they caught back up to the convoy.

CHAPTER 6

Next stop was an hour later when we reached a platoon of South Koreans who guarded three bridges on the Ia Drang River. O'Riley, with one of his private supply trucks, also stopped. This was one of his supply contacts. He wanted to double check his supply list. Driving up we were met with friendly faces, all waving. Three convoy trucks turned off and dropped off an entire loaded assortment of food and a hundred gallons of gas, ammunition, medical supplies, and whatever else they needed. Today was just a drop-off; they didn't leave any trucks. Lieutenant Anderson, O'Riley's second in command who was from Special Forces, spoke Korean with Sergeant O'Riley and Tony Lee, off to the side. Tony Lee was their Korean driver, a devoted Korean officer and a self-appointed supply clerk. They were talking over items they wanted to change, buy, or trade for. O'Riley was greeted by an old friend, the captain of the Korean's White Horse division. The Blue Dragon was the other Korean division that we worked with. They were mercenaries, paid by the US. Their ages varied from very young to very old. Smiling and enjoying the morning air, the Korean captain took everyone over to an open fire where O'Riley and his crew sat and had a conversation, watching the three cooks make fried rice with red onions, with coffee boiling on a rock.

Gathered together for breakfast, we were welcome to eat

with the Korean soldiers. They had a ten-foot-long python that had been cut open and they were preparing. This was a delicacy. If it was cooked right, it would melt in your mouth and leave you hungry for more. The outside kitchen firepit stove was aways busy; Korean soldiers were coming in to give their greetings and get breakfast. The ten-foot snake was a special feast the night patrol brought in just hours ago from the lowlands. The meat would only last two days, at the most. It was the equivalent of a tenderloin steak and was cooked with fried red onions; Koreans loved red onions. They offered us a large plate full. There was more than enough for everyone.

O'Riley and Tony Lee talked to the Korean captain while Anderson pulled boxes of a variety of alcohol out of the back of their truck. Then shaking hands, O'Riley said, "We can't stay long. We have to catch up with the rest of the vehicles."

The next stop was the mountain village of A Yun Pa and the Ba River, occupied with Special Forces and some Green Beret. These two platoons had been out on point with the South Vietnamese soldiers and had told Captain Shorts on the radio about what they had seen. Troops were engaged in fighting for the hill several miles away. The VC were out in force, the field radio traffic very heavy, all coming out of the Ia Drang Valley. Outposts were being hit day and night. This was only ten miles farther down on Highway 14 from the LZ Snowy Mountain.

The Green Beret were with a half dozen scouts and two or three squads of Montagnard troops on patrol. They set up a mobile listening post with night vision goggles. Always moving three or four times a night, they scouted the landscape that overlooked the valley below. Captain Shorts had agreed to meet up with them. A half dozen scouts with a field radio were on a hillside watching and waiting for us. This was a drop-off for much-needed supplies. We didn't know where they were but the scouts were watching the road and would tell us when to pull over and do the drop-off. Captain Shorts called out the names of two drivers to do the supply drop.

He told Burnie, the driver of the gun truck Whiskey Train, to drop off with them and stand guard. These were the units that watched the Ho Chi Minh Trail. Using the Montagnard patrols for their eyes and ears, the small patrol units only gathered information; they did not engage, if possible. Radio conversations were kept short and in a low voice. Scouts were reporting heavy troop movement with supplies and reinforcements. Much more traffic that week. The Special Forces reported that we were in the middle of a large troop movement all around us. No one called in intelligence at night. The NVA had captured some of our field radios and would be listening in.

All of the small LZ firebases were in total blackout all night. They had called for more backup. They wanted some tanks from the 1st Calvary (a base above Pleiku, in Dak To) and everybody wanted more air support. At this point Captain Shorts told everyone to be prepared. "All gun trucks, bring down your field radio antenna and send up a green and yellow flag with the American flag." That meant to get ready for anything.

A return call came back. "It's been done. We're flying our colors."

The convoys kept moving on. The Iron Butterfly, with Jerry Jeff at the wheel, called back to Chico.

"Should I drop back for the rearguard reinforcement?"

Chico gave them the okay.

Jerry Jeff downshifted and went into a power slide. He did a fast U-turn out of the convoy, going back slowly, moving alongside the other trucks. Watching as the Iron Butterfly moved past, those in the convoy noticed smoke coming out of the driver's window. You could only see the driver's helmet and part of his arm. You had to look hard and believe there was somebody living inside all that smoke.

Jerry Jeff was a chain smoker when his hands were free. When he was driving and wanted to enjoy a smoke, he put a small cigar up each one of his nostrils and lit them. This was just the way he smoked, whether he was driving or not. When he wanted to inhale, he nodded his head yes and then inhaled deeply. When he wanted to get rid of the ashes, he shook his head no. To keep the smoke out of his eyes, he kept the window down.

Driving back past the length of the convoy, Jerry Jeff slid sideways in the road then moved up, eye to eye with Chico, topside in the gun box. I was eye to eye with Tiny, who gave us the coyote howl. Jerry Jeff, in full control of the vehicle, gave us the peace sign; his facial expression looked like an old, smiling walrus. I was in the cargo bay with radio man Steamer. Their orders were to stay in formation and not to move in the convoy. The field radios were alive, all crews talking over the road ahead.

The talk was about the reports and troop movements. Everyone was watching the hilltops. We were going into a trap. Our job was to control the roads in the Central Highlands, a very rugged no man's land, filled with small villages along streams that were accessible by foot pass only. There was only one road in and out. It was the NVA's private domain. It was also the highway to the Ho Chi Minh Trail. Mang Yang Pass was our one main highway for our weapons and airpower to keep the Vietcong back. It was just a logging road until the Army Corps of Engineers brought in caterpillars, bulldozers, and earthmovers. The local logging people up here were still cutting two-hundred-year-old teak and mahogany trees by hand, then dragging them off the mountain with teams of elephants. The trees were then loaded onto old American trucks and transported down to the ocean to be exported.

Captain Shorts put out a call: "All trucks begin speeding up."

The gun trucks, being lighter and smaller, could out-turn everyone as if it was a NASCAR race. They were jockeying for position. Sergeant O'Riley and his crew were driving an 18-wheeler flatbed, which they traded for or had temporarily borrowed. They had also five-fingered a forklift, which they claimed the Air Force didn't need. In other words, the Airforce had left it unlocked. They had been planning tonight's raid for weeks. It was the US Army personnel who knew all about how to beg, borrow, or steal. We called it scrounging. The troops of the Central Highlands were all good at scrounging, maybe even be the best. With no rules, no one looked twice and didn't concern themselves by asking many questions.

O'Riley was on his field radio to Captain Shorts. The two old soldiers were talking over each other's checklist. Scheffler was talking to Captain Shorts, telling him tonight was a SOS mission, "Search Out and Steal."

The captain turned his attention back to the road and the oncoming attack we were going toward at full speed.

Shorts called O'Riley. "When do you want to leave in the morning?"

"You want something, don't you," O'Riley replied.

"There are a few things I could use."

"Sure. What do you need?"

"A minigun and some medical supplies for Doc Murray," Shorts said. "The minigun is not for me; it's for the Batmobile."

"I might be able to find one." O'Riley smiled and looked over to his business partners traveling with him, Tony Lee and Lieutenant Anderson. Anderson stood up on the seat in their 18-wheeler with a pair of binoculars watching the hilltop to the side and in front of them. (They had taken the roof off the cab.) We were coming to the Vietcong's favorite place to ambush. We knew what was about to hit us.

Sergeant O'Riley wanted to talk to Scheffler one more time about tonight's duty roster/work assignment for the Air Force and Navy's supply base. This was a big trip. Sometimes the 573 went to smaller supply ports closer to the 573, like in De Nang – a Marine supply base – or Quin Yan – an Army supply base and also one of our vacation spots.

After talking with Scheffler, Captain Shorts got on the squawk box again and wanted a count of vehicles. Then he called O'Riley to find out how many vehicles O'Riley wanted to use that night. The captain gave a quick call to the radioman on the SS Alabama, Richard, who reported that everyone was moving. "It's a go!"

The freight train was fully assembled and rolling down Mang Yang Pass. Crews started to add JP4 jet fuel to their diesel fuel, which you could see from the small flames coming out of the mufflers.

This was not very precise; they just poured the nitro in until the engine sounded as if it were about to blow up. All Army vehicles were built to withstand almost anything. All the crews knew what was waiting for them. The worst roads, all downhill, difficult hairpin downturns, which were even more difficult on the way back fully loaded.

Over the years the Vietcong and NVA took control by slowly moving in and reinforcing all the high points with inground bunkers connected by small foot passes only wide enough for two people to walk along. The VC preferred the hilltops so they could look down. Their road followed the hillside and cliffs. Falling trees and some branches had been cut back to keep the pass open. Everything else was almost totally untouched by humans.

In a few miles the convoy would drop into Dead Man's Straightaway. Before that, we called the road "Cliff-Hanging Curves." All the trucks had to gear down and follow the edge of the cliff. Going downhill the road became so narrow it could only be used by one vehicle at a time. Looking down over the side, coming out of the morning fog were two Huey helicopters moving south up the valley at tree-top level. We couldn't hear them, and we could just barely see them, running hundreds of feet below us, almost straight down. They looked like toys coming up the center of the valley. When they finally reached us, one of the Hueys, Dust Devil, came up to road level into the first-dawn light, sunlight reflecting off the rotary blades.

Along the steep hillside it moved forward to the front of the column of trucks. It was about to get serious.

Chapter 7

These choppers were our first line of attack and defense; they plowed the road from the air. In the morning light we saw yellow and green tracers coming toward our lead trucks, small arms fire from 50-caliber automatic Russian weapons. The North Vietnamese were getting warmed up, firing down, getting their range. The lead gun truck returned fire. All the gun truck snipers were on the field radio, calling out positions to fire at and claiming sure kills.

Stopping was not an option; we had to drive into the firefight. For the next hour the road would be fought for. On the right side it was almost straight up a hillside covered in large trees and boulders. On the left side, the landscape dropped off to what looked like a thousand feet of all cliffs. If we hit North Vietnamese with an airstrike, they simply ran into caves and bunkers, bomb shelters with mud floors and ceilings made of one-foot, heavily reinforced concrete. I heard Special Forces talk about being up there, going through entire compounds underground stairways leading up and down to three levels of living quarters and supply storage. Special Forces personnel always believed they were being watched from a distance; they weren't alone.

Charlie's scouts had spotted us coming and called in our convoy. They had been waiting for us to arrive. They were pouring across the border again. Months ago Special Forces and army units with Montagnard scouts were up on the hilltops, sealing off all the entrances with explosives. The VC were back and starting again, this time with a full regiment. They were rebuilding their underground bunkers. Many hills were actually small villages, all of them with two or more long tunnels for coming and going.

Captain Short and Sergeant Scheffler were taking fire. They quickly dropped back, moving the Batmobile behind Instant Hell and Ground Pounder. Short was calling to all gunners. "Keep sending out rounds. Lite 'em up!"

Return fire from the American tracers were red and orange. Ground Pounder had three 50 calibers with all firepower to the front. Instant Hell had two sets of side-by-side 60s, with two Ma Deuces – two M2s, a loaded and ready single-shot 50-caliber sniper rifle. We called it a hand cannon.

Ground Pounder was still moving forward at top speed. Flunky was gritting his teeth and holding on to the rear-corner Ma Deuce. He lit up the hilltop at two o'clock. All the gun trucks were putting out return fire and receiving incoming fire. As we moved farther into the straightaway, there was returning small arms fire coming down the length of the convoy. Three rocket-propelled grenades (RPG) rounds were fired badly in our direction and just broke the air – we saw the smoke and felt the RPG as it passed overhead.

They adjusted, aimed, and fired again, one then another, hitting Instant Hell. The gun box was torn open, taking out the back corner, the lower portion just above the rear wheels. Farther up the hill two more RPG from another position were in the air. A fully loaded flatbed with scrap metal was hit, the blast sending the load over the side and down the cliff. It was Big Ray.

Big Ray bailed out and saved himself, bouncing off the ground face down. He looked up to see the last of his truck disappear. But he was all right. He got to his feet and ran to the side of the road before he got run over. Then he ran up to the next 18-wheeler and jumped on board on the driver side, crawling up into the front compartment with the driver, who was firing an M79. Big Ray moved over to the passenger side and picked up a 60 caliber and returned fire. The Army would have to send a Chinook to recover the iron off the 18-wheeler. We never left any metal in the field. The locals or the NVC would melt it down and turn it into a weapon or get it running again.

Another flatbed was hit but was still moving. It was another load of scrap iron, which bounced off the flatbed on both sides. Farther back a well-aimed rocket tore through a tanker, blowing it totally open on both sides, cutting it almost in half. The NVA were up there in numbers. Ground Pounder took on another rocket. It exploded on the armor siding, taking out four feet of the corner, taking with it one 50 caliber. A second one hit Instant Hell on the upper right corner of the gun box. Its half-inch steel wall protection was cut open and peeled back like a banana.

Mortars now dropped down in six or seven places. More yellow and green tracers from the hilltops. Small arms bounced off our armor; it sounded like large stones knocking together. More shells passed overhead making a hissing noise with a shock wave, popping our ear drums. All second drivers in the 18-wheelers were returning fire with M60s or M79s.

The NVA knew the easiest way to stop the convoy was to shoot out our tires. One of the last trucks, another tanker, had been hit just behind the tractor's rear axle, disconnecting the empty tanker from the tractor. It slid off and to the right, rolled over once, then came to rest on its side, leaving just barely enough room for the rest of the convoy to keep moving.

As the fighting continued, the second Huey helicopter came from the valley below. Keeping in line with the first helicopter on their left, both door gunners started firing. The door gunner on Dust Devil strapped himself down with a safety harness so he could stand completely outside with a mounted machine gun loaded and ready. The second Huey was Black Nights. They returned fire to the hilltops straight ahead. The Black Nights' pilot called in his firing mission, telling Dust Devil, in a loud voice, "Move over; we're coming in hot."

Each pilot sent out three or four missiles, all hitting the hillside in a straight line just in front of Ground Pounder and Instant Hell.

Dust Devil opened up again on the hilltop, then moved down to the roadside and kept looking for any kind of movement. It was the chopper's job to lay down maximum firepower just ahead of the convoy in the "killing field" just above the ground. This was to try and keep the VC from shooting out our tires. Both gun trucks and choppers were running parallel, eyes to eye. The choppers slowed down and were watching the gun trucks on their right side. The truck and choppers were only forty feet apart. The pilots moved their birds in and out, following the cliff edge, almost as though he was in another vehicle in the passing lane. Dust Devil's door gunner opened up with a long burst of 60-caliber fire. Still eye to eye, he smiled at the gun trucks, which were taking fire.

Lefty, driving Instant Hell, signaled to his radiomen and co-driver, Bogard. He quickly climbed out of the gun box, over the steel protection, and down into the driver's seat and took control of the vehicle. The gun trucks had removed their hard-top roofs. Lefty was holding onto the steering wheel with three fingers on his right hand and trying to load his weapon with his left. They had installed a machine gun on the driver's side door, an M60.

Bogard yelled, "I've got it!"

With that Lefty opened up the breach and inserted the bandolier. Holding onto the driver's door, he looked for a target. He sent out a full bandolier of fire into the hillside where he saw NVA shooting down at them.

Chico, on the SS Alabama, radioed in, "We've taken two rockets!" One had slammed square in the front upper corner of the gun box and had taken out one of the 106s, knocking it to the floor. Smoking Joe was almost blown over the side. He was hit and didn't respond on the radio. The upper part of the gun box was torn apart.

Chico called out for some Cobra helicopters, "Get some snakes in the air!"

Cobras were smaller, faster choppers that had more firepower: missiles, rockets, and mini-guns.

A third round hit again, this time in the center of the back of the gun box, bouncing off and leaving a dent. Smoking Joe tried to move on the deck, rolling over and looking at the sky. He raised his right hand, his eyes focused. "I'm not dying here." He was coming around. Smoking Joe talked to Chico on the radio, but he didn't know where he was. For a minute Smoking Joe was calling out the members of his crew.

To his right, the 106, which had landed on top of his leg, was fully loaded and had to be disarmed. The 105 in the center and the other 106 were still ready and loaded on their mountings. He found his helmet and spit out a mouthful of blood onto his flak jacket, which was ripped open. On his hands and knees, he crawled to the other side of the cargo bay. Shells were whistling overhead, some hitting the inside and bouncing around. He stayed down but started to think straight and move fast.

Still more yellow and green tracers were hitting inside the gun box. The entire convoy was taking direct incoming shots. More North Vietnamese firing from the hillside to the front and all along the length of the convoy. It was a death trap.

Smoking Joe spit out more blood. He looked around and saw Richard in the back of the gun box. He wasn't moving. Keeping down on his hands and knees, he moved over to him. Richard's eyes were closed but he was alive and breathing. Looking him over, he decided he had had the air knocked out of him. His helmet was dented, and he possibly had a concussion.

Smoking Joe grabbed him by the shirt collar and pulled, kneeling and pulling over to the last working gun position, a M2 ready for action. Smoking Joe reloaded the 50 caliber as more tracers hit the truck. Smoking Joe opened up the Ma Deuce with returning fire. He put his hand on the trigger and kept it there, his fire pattern moving from the rear to the front, then back to the center. Still cursing and spitting out a small amount of blood, he stopped the incoming fire that was coming at him, then spit out more blood. He felt his rib cage. The lower half of his flak jacket was gone, but there was no time to think about himself. He put his finger on the trigger and lit up the hillside.

Slowly he brought the weapon to the center, then reloaded and looked for another target. There was no turning around. The VC intended to take out the lead and the rear vehicle, trapping the convoy and destroying all of us. In the front gun truck, Lefty opened his door wide and reloaded the 60 caliber, which was bolted onto the driver's door facing out. He pushed the driver's door all the way forward and stepped out to the edge of the running board. The gun truck bounced through a long pothole. Lefty bounced around and almost fell off, holding onto the bandolier with one hand, swinging his right hand in the air. His left foot was the only thing keeping him alive.

Bogard managed to grab hold of his flak jacket and he pulled his crazy partner back.

Bogard yelled, "You know you and your family were chronically disturbed with a history of mental illness."

"I knew that ten years ago," Lefty replied back.

"Then we'll all go down together!"

With a big half-crazy smile, Lefty opened up again shouting, "We're coming to get me some road!"

Bogard was doing his best to drive and hold onto his friend.

~ JAMES VOELKER ~

Incoming fire was still coming down. We knew we needed more air support, and we called out for some.

The Huey chopper pilot immediately replied, "The snakes are in the air. Coming up behind you!"

CHAPTER 8

Black Nights, flying side-by-side with the convoy, gave us the high sign. He fired to the right and over the top of the convoy, which was getting incoming fire from halfway up the hillside. The 18-wheeler's radio men were firing 79s at the same time. Lefty reloaded with both hands, Bogard holding onto his collar.

"Listen, mother fucker, get back in the truck!"

Lefty replied, "One more round!"

He opened up again, firing on the hilltop, then saw more rockets in the air. The gun truck bounced in and out of a pothole. Lefty lost his balance again. Holding onto the door handle, he was saved again by Bogard, this time pulling him all the way into the truck.

On the field radio coming from the lead gun truck, Ground Pounder's radioman heard a voice. It was Flunky in the gun box just behind him.

"Sink's been hit! He's wounded in the neck and shoulders. He appears to be all right, but he wants to lay down."

Other wounded were reported on the radios. Farther back, more were calling in with severely wounded and dead. The door gunner in Black Night gave us another thumbs up. He nodded his head and pointed to the back of the convoy as if he wanted everyone to look up. Coming in at full speed were two Cobra choppers. A call came in. "Snakes in the air!" They had arrived and were on the attack.

The new voice came over the squawk box. He introduced himself. "This is Doctor Death, pilot of Snake Eyes, coming in for a kill."

Two gun ships were coming forward about three hundred yards apart. One behind the other at full speed only twenty feet above the trucks, moving up the convoy, then dropping down even closer. The Cobra pilots had been staying back until the North Vietnamese soldiers gave away their position. At this point the pilot opened up with Gatling guns, turning the air above the convoy into a wall of yellow and orange flames, with a reddish glow. Firing thousands of rounds per minute, the brass cartridges by the hundreds were raining down on the open trucks below.

Casings were everywhere, some down the backs of the driver's and crew's flak jackets and uniforms. They were still hot and smoking with the smell of gunpowder. The Cobra kept firing, only ten feet above the lead vehicles. At this point Snake Eyes sped up, continuing to fire. Passing over the lead truck, the Cobra dropped down to only five feet off the road. Moving forward, he brought the nose up.

Then he launched a handful of missiles straight ahead. The pilot pulled the throttle to the left and sent out the last pattern of rockets. Continuing forward and climbing to forty feet, he slowed down and turned the Gatling gun into the hillside, moving like the minute hand on the clock. The other Cobra, the Green Hornet, was coming in at full speed, doing the same, raining twice as much hot ammo cartridges onto the convoy. You couldn't see the floor from all the brass cartridges so the drivers had to open their door and use their feet to push the empty cartridges away from the gas pedal and brake.

The Green Hornet climbed to one hundred feet, the copilot feeding information to the front pilot, one-by-one picking out individual targets and stopping almost all enemy fire. Snake Eyes was now firing white tracers, which was the signal to the gunship that it was running out of ammunition; it needed to go back to base to reload. The convoy began moving into a steep downgrade turn. The trucks were slowing down to almost a walk. One Huey was bringing up the rear to support Snake Eyes. It moved to the front of the convoy, passing overhead and going up the hilltop, searching for targets.

The field radios were alive, everyone putting out the word where to look next. Green Hornet moved to the rear and farther up the mountainside, sending fire into suspected spots. After a long burst of 60-caliber rounds, the gunship turned to go back to the front of the convoy. Suddenly, a string of yellow tracers from a Russian 50 caliber hit the side of the helicopter, taking out the pilot, sending it dropping down toward the cliffs in an out-of-control spiral. The copilot managed to straighten out the chopper and turned away from the cliffs, limping for home.

There were still twenty-five more vehicles moving along into the downhill turns. Inside the cargo bay of Ground Pounder, they had Sink lying down and had called for advice from Doc Murray, who was one of our best field medics.

"His neck wound is more severe than we thought," Flunky said. "Part of his shoulder bone's been shattered and some of it's gone. A 50-caliber round ripped through his flak jacket and his shoulder bone, just missing his heart."

Doc Murray replied, "Keep him quiet, and stop the bleeding."

Flunky was on his knees, cutting open the first aid kit, talking to him as if it was his kid brother. He did his best to doctor up Sink's neck wound. Sink was struggling for air and was breathing lighter and lighter. Flunky got on the radio to Doc Murray for more medical instructions.

"Doc, he's hardly breathing!"

"Stop the bleeding. Put him on his side so he can spit out the blood. If at all possible, put something in the air vent, even if you use your hand or your fingers."

With that Flunky sat back down and tried again to stop the bleeding. Sink looked at Flunky and moved his lips, wanting to talk. He raised up his hand to Flunky's shoulder, then it dropped onto Flunky's arm.

Flunky watched, then looked up to the sky. He took hold of Sink's hand and felt his friend go cold. Sink's hand was shaking, his spirit was leaving, he could see it in his eyes. He knew it was going to happen, but he thought he had more time. When someone died right in front of you, you always wanted more time. When it ended with a close friend, you realized this person took some of yourself with him. Sink took a piece of Flunky with him.

Sink's eyes glazed over but still were open. Both his legs were straightened out. Sink looked at Flunky, his lips had stopped moving, and he was no longer gasping for air. His mouth opened up just a little bit as if to say goodbye. With a small exhale, Sink gave up his life. He had taken his last look at the world, his last breath. Sink was still looking at Flunky as if he was just going to sleep for a couple minutes. Flunky pulled the rain poncho over him and tucked it under his body to keep him warm. Then he took another rain poncho and covered his face.

"Good night. Stay warm."

Then Ground Pounder came to life. Flunky yelled into the headphones to the other crewmen, telling everyone, "Light 'em up."

Flunky got back to his weapon, the single-shot 50 caliber. Things were about to get worse; he was looking for revenge. More fire was coming down the entire length of the convoy. Flunky sent out three rounds with his 50 caliber, looking for the next target. The Geneva convention said you couldn't use 50 calibers on people, but the rules went out the window in this situation.

Overhead, Snake Eyes was taking a hit in the rear compartment

~ MANG YANG PASS ~

and had an electrical fire. Captain Shorts called for med flight but heard nothing back. They wouldn't come into these valleys. If med flight came in, they wouldn't come out. All the helicopters had disappeared.

Captain Shorts was now calling the Air Force for a bombing mission. There was more return fire now, only coming from the very tops of the cliffs, green and yellow tracers coming down.

The sharpshooters started using their single-shot, 50-caliber sniper rifles, which we called hand cannons. The Browning 50 calibers had been rebuilt in the armory and reassembled with telescopes into a new tool for the sharpshooters. All the gun crews had one or two on each vehicle. With this weapon, the sharpshooters called themselves zappers.

Scanning the hilltops, looking for moving targets, the hand cannons were deadly at long-range. The gun trucks' sharpshooters were putting out rounds, knocking down the enemy as they tried to move. As we came to a large turn and downgrade, the sharp shooters continued to hit their targets. Captain Shorts had a pair of binoculars and was calling out targets as we came out of the turn, into a straightaway and another downgrade.

We heard bugles, which were used by the North Vietnamese regulars to signal each other. We looked up to the higher elevations and saw North Vietnamese flags and faces that were not there a minute ago. All the firing stopped. Dozens of North Vietnamese were looking down and waving their weapons. It was like a parade, no effort to move off the edge. The North Vietnamese were very confident and were standing their ground. Five North Vietnamese field commanders with dozens of lieutenants and other soldiers kept coming to the edge and looking down, many waving their AK-47s. More flags were coming to the edge, some unit flags from the North and Viet Cong flags from the south. No one was moving. It was a show of arms. It was a game, and someone had called for a timeout. They were just standing and enjoying the view. The NVA regiment was in position in their stronghold and was not going to allow us to pass through their domain. These field units all looked as though they had traveled a very long way, dressed in combat uniforms, brown helmets with red stars. It was the Ghost Army and its Ghost General, Vo Nguyen Giap. They got their name because they would take us on, then disappear for weeks, then months later would reappear.

There was no movement of any kind from the NVA, only standing and watching. They could easily be rolling large stones into our vehicles. Just their very presence meant trouble. They were looking down, as if overseeing their own parade of troops.

Captain Shorts and General Giap saw each other, both turning their heads with distrust. Some of the old drivers on their third tour in-country had heard about other encounters with Giap and his regiment from different parts of the Mang Yang Pass. A handful of drivers had seen him and lived to tell about it. He had a new army. His troops were in a battle some months ago and took a very heavy beating.

General Giap had 500 or 600 field-hardened troops from the 304 and 320 Divisions coming across on the Ho Chi Minh Trail, straight out of Cambodia, hooking up with the 17th company of Viet Minh. General Giap could have wiped out the entire convoy with a wave of his hand. The Chinese book of war told us a great field commander's name and all his glory of success in the field would live on for decades. Genghis Khan's writings were older than that. He still talked to us, giving advice to his generals and captains for hundreds if not thousands of years to come, written on rice paper scrolls. The Chinese warlord Genghis Khan talked to his commanders and soldiers on horseback. He was a great field commander and leader of all his troops. He would be remembered with honor for his knowledge to command. 'Know your enemy troops and commander as well as he knows his own regiments. You need to know what stands behind you and what stands in

~ MANG YANG PASS ~

front of you. This will declare your victory making a commander famous and give him glory long after their battles, making him immortal in the eyes of his homeland.'

The hilltop was silent. It was scary and made everyone uneasy. The trip back up Mang Yang Pass would be all trouble. The North Vietnamese started to space themselves out, three, maybe four to a group. Moving along, around, and behind boulders and trees, they occasionally popped out with a rifle. They were headhunting, looking for an opening shot at our CO. All the gun truck sharpshooters shot their hand cannons before the NV had a chance to get off a shot at the captain. The 50-caliber hand cannon was a superior weapon, even though it was handmade from used parts. When it hit a man, it tore him apart.

The NVA started firing again, sending a number of RPGs raining down in front of the convoy, blowing up the road and making it even slower, bouncing into and over the potholes.

A call went out. We want the helicopters back.

Tiny from the SS Alabama announced, "I can see three choppers coming in from the west."

The snakes were coming back. The first two gun ships opened up along the hillsides. Captain Shorts was on the radio to the rearguard, the SS Alabama. Shouting out to Sergeant Chico, "We need a fire mission in the upper position with beehives!"

A beehive canister turned a 105 artillery piece into a giant shotgun; each canister contained thousands of winged nails three inches long.

Chico called back, "No shot!"

Then another call came from radioman Richard. "No shot!"

Chico, Smoking Joe, and Tiny needed time to bring the truck in line. A short minute later Chico was on the radio to his cargo bay crewmen, Tiny, and second gunner, Smoking Joe, who began turning the barrel around. They aimed the 105 to where the North Vietnamese flag and General Vo Nguyen Giap was last seen.

57

"I'll light them up in ten seconds."

As the truck moved around a large turn, they saw their target. "Send it!" Chico called out.

With that, beehive rounds started hitting the stone hillside cliffs, sending the small metal arrows into the trees. Some rounds went into stones, flying off, and many dropped down on the trucks below. The North Vietnamese were saving their ammunition and had disappeared like ghosts. They knew on our return trip the Americans would be overloaded.

On the cliff tops you could see dozens of North Vietnamese or Viet Cong regulars running and moving along with the convoy. The NVA soldiers had been waiting for a chance to get in a shot at the Batmobile. They wanted the bounty money. These were the Viet Cong sharpshooters. The bounty money was more than a year's pay for just one of them. All six of the gun truck zappers had their hand cannons putting out rounds and were dropping the Viet Cong before they could get a shot out, targeting the hilltops with deadly accuracy.

They were hitting their targets then calling in sure kills and their next firing position. The single-shot M2 had become a valuable weapon. Tiny, following along the hillside, was weapon-ready and loaded. The freight train headed into another bad turn, all downhill. It was only twenty more miles before we were out of the mountain pass, but now we had air protection. All at once the North Vietnamese disappeared. They were moving to their bunkers and caves; their scouts had alerted them.

Overhead two Navy F4 Phantom planes provided air cover, one on each side of the road. Higher up three F105 Thunderchiefs were heading up the pass for a strike. They dropped down to 1000 feet and checked us out. A push-pull Cessna (a prop job with one motor in the front, one in the back) was in contact with the Batmobile. He wanted to pinpoint his target for an air strike. He told the CO, "It's time to unleash hell."

~ MANG YANG PASS ~

The last of the convoy was still slowly coming around the big hill and downturn. Like most vehicles, the 18-wheeler had taken multiple hits. Shot up badly and slowly moving, the last 18-wheelers drove out and away from the drop zone, doing all it could to clear out of danger.

Captain Shorts told all the other truck crews to watch for rolling thunder (an air strike) in their rearview mirrors, but not to stop through the last turns. The SS Alabama had turned their 106 and 105 barrels, sending out rounds to the hilltops behind them, marking the drop zone. The Cessna saw the gun fire and called in the location to the F105s. The Thunderchiefs had turned around and were coming in for the first air strike.

The bombers dropped down out of the sky and became visible. At 3500 feet they dropped their bombs, blowing up the hilltops and dropping large amounts of stones and tree stumps down onto the road behind them.

Shorts called the Army Corps of engineers for repairs. We would need this road open for our return trip. The worst part of the road was over. Everyone could take off their helmets. We were out of the Mang Yang Pass.

CHAPTER 9

*I*t was a different world seeing flat roads, civilians walking, some families moving along a dirt path along the side of the road, which was surrounded by palm trees and overgrown waterways, the rice paddy fields becoming larger every few miles. The convoy was now up to full speed. Captain Shorts on the radio: "Put up the green flag but keep your speed limit down. We'll be coming into Buon Ho and Mamasans trading post.

"All you lunatic drivers, no running farmers and their animals off the road with your trucks, as you do in the Highlands!"

The captain knew not to trust any of these guys farther than he could throw a grenade.

"I've put a call in for medical backup so keep your eyes peeled.

"We'll make all repairs tonight, do all the tire changes in Cam Ranh. Anyone ending up in the MP's jail will stay there. No exceptions."

Everybody watched for Red Cross choppers. A call came in; they were five minutes out.

The captain called for antennas to be brought down and red flags attached. "Those in need, meet up with the medical choppers."

Several flares were shot off, giving the choppers a welcome, and we radioed a report on the men. Several men had died from their wounds. All anyone could do was wrap them up in rain ponchos. Sink was still in the cargo bay of Ground Pounder with Flunky. On the Whiskey Train Johnny Reb didn't make it either. He was one of the best drivers in the convoy but today he gave the ultimate price and lost. Sink and Johnny Reb came in country together and had only been with the company over ten months. Now they were being stretched out and their corpses moved onto a rain poncho.

Flunky stayed with Sink and talked with him as if nothing had happened. He pulled the metal dog tag off his right boot. Sink and three other men had their R&R all planned out. On Whiskey Train Shotgun Eddie pulled the dog tag off of Johnny Reb's right leg. They would write to each family and tell them about their last day together.

The medical helicopters were dropping down, landing in the center of the road. A call went out, "Up and down the line we need three blood types!"

Doc said, "Types A+, four, maybe more. One O and one, maybe two B-negative!" If you had that type of blood, you walked over and were told to lie down inside the helicopter. At that point they double-checked your dog tag, then brought up the severely wounded for a blood transfusion. These choppers were having a busy day. They ran out of everything; wounds were being bandaged with T-shirts.

No plasma left, these men couldn't wait; they needed help now, before the helicopters returned them to the hospital. I wanted to help a badly wounded gunner named Rocky. I walked over and rolled up the sleeve of my jungle fatigue but maybe it was too late. He wasn't moving and his eyes were closed. I felt so helpless. I couldn't take my eyes off him. You didn't have to give blood in a combat zone; it was your choice. I stretched out on the deck of the Huey. One of the chopper medics cleaned up my arm and the arm of another soldier waiting to give blood, then went on to his next personnel. Rocky was set down directly below me. Doc Murray hooked him up at once. He was a seventeen-year-old kid, a Puerto Rican from Big Daddy Virgo Rat. He had been shot just below his flak jacket. Doc had all his fingers wrapped and tied together with one of his shoestrings, his thumbs and fingers made into a "basket" that wouldn't come apart. Inside the basket he held his large intestine with a very large exit wound. He was still alive, and he started calling out in pain. Coughing up blood, his eyes were open slightly.

Doc Murray gave each man a very small drink of water. Watching the pipeline of blood moving into Rocky's arm, I looked down. It was all I could do. Blood from Rocky dripped down through his bandages. Dark red in color, dropping to the ground. It was soaked up by the parched dirt and was bringing in flies. *Is that Rocky's blood dripping or maybe mine passing through Rocky?* I thought.

Then Doc asked, "Are you feeling all right? Can you keep giving for another couple minutes?"

After being disconnected, I stepped over and went down on one knee next to Rocky. "You'll be fine. You're on your way home."

Then Rocky was carried over to the waiting Red Cross chopper.

On the other side of the helicopter, Chico was giving blood to Smoking Joe.

"On pay day I want something for this."

Smoking Joe looked at him and laughed. "I'll put you in my will and buy you a drink tonight."

Then Doc disconnected them, and they walked away still swearing at each other "Another pint of your blood and I'll be talking like someone from Long Island. I'll have a big mouth and bad teeth and snort through my nose like a horse."

"Listen, asshole, you're the only one with my blood type so we have to keep one another alive. Besides, you're buying more than one drink tonight."

Looking around they saw other men were doing the same.

~ MANG YANG PASS ~

Some men were running to help the walking wounded. Crews from Ground Pounder and Instant Hell all started walking over to help Doc Murray, who had given the okay to bring Sink off the floor of the cargo bay. Four men joined in to help carry him to the assembly area for the dead. Other gun trucks were doing the same – their last walk together. Sink was one of four who unfortunately didn't make it. All were given a combat funeral procession. Wrapped up in a rain poncho, the crew was like their family. Sink's crew and other gun truck crews carried their own across the road, which now had a trail of red blood.

The medical team wanted Sink in the third Huey chopper with the other dead, the last bird out. The badly wounded were the first to lift off; walking wounded who didn't need as much medical attention would be the second bird to fly up. The first chopper off would land at the Army hospital and, if needed, transport to the Navy ship hospital. After the choppers were loaded up, the first two Hueys moved off. The last chopper still hadn't started its jet engine. Troops of men just stood around. No one saluted. Other men came up to pay their respects to one of their own.

I went over to Sink to say my last goodbye. Flunky handed me Sink's dog tag. "I'm going to return it to your family in Connecticut, I promise. I'll get this to your family. I have their address. I will tell them how the day started and ended. I will tell them about your bravery."

Flunky walked over. "It's time to suck it up."

Captain Shorts and Scheffler came over too, taking off their helmets and standing with their men. The CO made the sign of the cross on himself, closed the doors, and signaled for the move-off. Shorts and Scheffler walked off with their heads down, one behind the other. Nothing was said. For a couple of minutes, all the convoy crews watched the last chopper lift off. In four or five hours the day would be done; the hard part was over.

Chapter 10

The convoy continued on down country to Cam Ranh Bay. Everyone was on the radio, talking about their next stop at Mamasans supermarket. It was on a turnoff to Highway 27, east, over the Da Dang River, then five miles to the corner of Q14 and Q27. It was a bakery and grocery store, and Mamason sold gas by the quart. She always had cold sodas, homemade hotdogs, and rice bread baking outside, with two tables under an army surplus tent. This stop gave the men time to think; in only a couple of hours or more they would be seeing the ocean.

Driving up to Mamasans, her people waved with greetings, coming out carrying merchandise they wished to sell, calling out with happy voices, eager to make a sale to their friends.

Sergeant O'Riley's truck pulled over and called to Mamasan and her family working that day. All went inside. Tony Lee carried some small wooden boxes. They were probably doing some money laundering. A short while later O'Riley and Tony Lee walked back out, still conversing with Mamasans and two partners. They were all standing around shaking their heads yes. Mamasan held up both hands and put out eight fingers and in English counted to seven. Tony Lee pointed to her eighth digit and held up his hands with eight fingers out.

With that, O'Riley had the shopping list that she was requesting. The crew were called back again to the road. Whiskey

~ MANG YANG PASS ~

Train was now assigned to be O'Riley's bodyguard. They moved out together and joined the convoy.

Hours later the train of vehicles could see the ocean. Traffic became heavier. The road changed to four lanes for miles. This was a busy harbor seaport, one of the busiest in the South China Sea. Most trucks on the road were headed directly to the dock for supplies. All branches of the service were here. Many Merchant Marine ships were waiting in the harbor to offload. Vehicles broke off of our convoy to different parts of the combined military base. The convoy all would reassemble later. The rest of the day was spent making repairs to turn around and be ready for tomorrow.

The badly damaged tankers and flatbeds would be replaced. The fuel tankers would all resupply. Flatbed trucks had to offload and were given directions and a map of the supplies on the base. Junk vehicles and planes were offloaded right on the waterfront junkyard. Then they were given directions and orders to load up new artillery pieces and thousands of rounds of artillery shells. Doc Murray rode along in a flatbed truck, and he periodically had it stop so he could look over the supply area for things of interest, especially hospital equipment.

The sun was going down and Sergeant O'Riley and his helpers were gathering together and sharing information and hand-drawn maps. Five of O'Riley's scouts were talking about what a great place this was; the harbor was overstocked with everything they needed in the Central Highlands. They were told they needed three to four weeks for the paperwork to process. They were finding quantities of each item on their want list, even other items they weren't expecting to find but were also willing to steal. They were still looking for the alcohol: Rum, Brandy, Johnnie Walk, Gin, beer.

Two Korean scouts had been casually mapping out the Navy supply base for the supplies they wanted. They were looking to grab one or two new vehicles. Some of the base supply areas were shutting down for the day; many of the roads were dark and quiet. There were no guards to be seen, and empty vehicles were parked on the waterfront.

Doc Murray joined O'Riley's crew and was running along, making notes and maps. The crew was on the radio to the flatbed getaway truck. In a low voice they were calling O'Riley to a new location. Two scouts had gained entrance to a large repair building that had no fence. First Lieutenant Anderson had been driving around making his own map, sometimes getting out of the Jeep he just borrowed from the Navy.

He was now sneaking around, looking into windows or under canvases to identify items on the want list. Some items had just been unloaded that day. Many good items were on the harbor front pier. Generators were the first thing on the shopping list. Several scouts had located one good-sized diesel generator with some smaller ones on the Air Force base. They were still in wooden boxes, just taken off the ship. They had way too many.

Moving off, doing more patrols, the Korean soldiers also located some good prospects. Five brand-new two-and-a-half-ton trucks were lined up and ready for duty. One truck was put on the top of the list. This decreased their down time, which kept growing. Food and booze were always top of the list. They couldn't leave all that good food behind an eight-foot fence.

It was time. Sergeant O'Riley gave the order; his band of black-market outlaws were on the run. All were quite good with wrenches. Their first target, a brand-new diesel generator that the Air Force motor pool only used part-time; perfect for the first target.

Tony Lee and one of the other Koreans ran out in front with the radio for security; they were the "eyes and ears." They were ahead of the other crews, keeping in contact, calling in the best targets and a price they would sell this stuff at. All other crews were off scouting, signaling to each other with flashlights with red filters.

O'Riley, with two American lieutenants, were doing all the hands-on work on the generator, carefully detailing the project down to the last nut and bolt. Without a word, he dismantled all electrical and fuel lines, then loaded up the generator with a forklift. It was the first thing to be loaded onto the flatbed. The muffler was still warm with exhaust still coming out. This only took thirty minutes, so they put out a call for their next item.

Sergeant O' Riley had a different personality in the middle of his SOS mission. He turned into a brilliant juvenile delinquent with a smile to match. O'Riley and Anderson were in the flatbed moving up to the next call. Sitting in the front seat, they were talking about events coming up and the ones they pulled off last year and the year before when they almost got caught trying to steal an entire truckload of booze. Smiling at one another, they were talking about this being the last time.

"I'm going to retire, move to Montana, and buy a ranch on the Big Horn River," Anderson said.

O'Riley said, "I'm going home to Ireland."

At a very early age he signed up with the Irish Army, served good time, and left a few years later. O'Riley moved from the Irish Army into the England Royal Army for three years. Still a young man and quite skilled in mechanics and robbery, and the ability to keep a straight face, he enlisted for the third time, joining the American Army serving in Germany. This much we knew for sure. It was a story he loved telling.

"I'll go home to my little village, but I'd like a second home overlooking the harbor in Sydney.

"Nothin' like the nightlife in the Kings Cross."

With some gray hair, O'Riley was a little too old to be just a sergeant. Why did he wind up in the backcountry of Vietnam? He wasn't much of a fighter but very good at being self-sufficient.

He could make almost anything disappear and reappear with a forklift, and he was capable of running a mobile trading post. He had been in Vietnam four or five years. He knew everywhere and everyone. Some say he even traded with the North Vietnamese. He organized his own crew, which consisted of some very professional Koreans (officers in charge of troops and who had some pull), and his personal staff and associates, including two lieutenants who were members of Special Forces.

A call came in for him, a happy voice. It was Tony Lee. "Jackpot! A new truck and I started it. I'm moving up to my next SOS. Send up help."

Everyone was busy and waiting for the forklift. Three scouts were all standing in a circle, everyone holding a flashlight and a hand-drawn map, talking over and arguing about who claimed what or a price they would sell something they don't own. They were willing to stick their neck out for a profit.

They were still scouting the cargo on the dock that was just unloaded from the Merchant Marine ships hours ago. Tony Lee called in. He had three stops mapped out for some hard-to-find electronics, which had to be disconnected. Almost everything on the list took time to disassemble. They were thinking they needed a third truck. Three men were sent off for another two-and-a-half-ton on the dock, which they would hotwire and drive off.

Doc Murray called in and wanted help. He found the material he wanted and requested a truck. O'Riley called Tony Lee and one of his scouts to send the second new vehicle over to Doc's location.

Another call came in. One of the scouts requested the vehicle and help at their next target. The scouts had located an outback building and were waiting for more lights to go off and people to retire to bed.

Looking for bigger items, Tony Lee called in directions to bring in the flatbed and forklift, which O'Riley was driving. He was sneaking along the main road of the Navy supply base. Having done this before, it had become a favorite shopping center.

One of the scouts called in. "A fight broke out, right next to refrigerated units full of food." A fight broke out was code for they found a liquor cabinet.

While all this was going on, the gun crews were finishing fixing up the trucks for the convoy the next day, fueling up and getting them ready to roll. It was totally dark, and everyone had had a long day. Most of all they just wanted to forget about the friends they lost.

All six of the gun trucks had been welded back together. In many places the gun boxes had patches on top of patches for the third and fourth time. Some were adding metal roof plating for the trip back home. The drivers and sharpshooters, with the gunner crews, looked their vehicles over for the last time. They wanted to make sure the vehicles were ready for the road the next day.

All the gun truck crews were standing together and counting heads. Ten men in total who weren't seriously wounded were put on a medical flight and airlifted out to a military hospital or more than likely to a medical ship heading for the Philippines. If they died out at sea, their names wouldn't show up as casualties in Vietnam. We would never see them again. Hopefully, we would get a letter to know they made it, so we knew they were back home and where to send their personable items, if necessary.

Many tires were shot out. Three tanker trucks were destroyed, and two flatbeds had been pieced back together with parts from other old trucks. With the welding done, the repairs list was looked over. It was all going well. The first flatbeds were loaded with new artillery, ten vehicles were loaded down with brand new 8-inch howitzer barrels all chained down tightly for the trip back up to the 573. Other flatbeds were loaded down with an assortment of artillery shells and other military equipment, mainly other explosives for the artillery bases in the Central Highlands.

All old and new trucks were back and all in line to fuel up and be loaded. The gunners were working on their own hand cannons. They were all talking about the price for selling one.

Flunky said, "I'm going to ask two hundred cash."

Lefty added, "Me too."

"That's not enough," Cowboy said. "But then no one is as good as me, so it doesn't matter what gun they're using. I got eight kills today, for sure."

"Bull shit. I got five," McNulty said. "I'm keepin' my cannon. I need to get more of those gooks on the way back. They need to pay." He pointed to the bandage on his arm.

Burnie and Shotgun Eddie brought a couple hand cannons out of Whiskey Train and set them on the ground.

"Four for me," I said. "But we need twice as much ammo on the way back. We need more firepower than ever."

Many heads nodded around the group.

"But we have to have a demonstration," Burnie said, "show them what they can do before we start talking about price."

"Great idea!" Shotgun Eddie said.

Chico's crew walked over to the NCO club. The long day over, they wanted some fun and food. NCO club was a good place for a hot meal and a cold drink. Steamer and Ammatwozeo carried a hand cannon with them to the club. Jerry Jeff carried the stand for the weapon.

"I've got a scotch on the rocks with my name on it," Steamer said.

Ammatwozeo said, "With a beer chaser."

They high-fived each other.

"At home Brandy Old-Fashioned is my drink," I say.

"That's a woosy drink," Chico said. "Whiskey straight up is what men drink."

~ *MANG YANG PASS* ~

Ten new replacements had just arrived and had their gear thrown in one of the trucks. The young gunner crew agreed to come along to the NCO club.

Cowboy and Lefty set their hand cannons on top of the bar, eager to show them off and to possibly sell. It took two men to carry one. These weapons had no polished brass. They were recycled parts, but the best long-range, customized rifle. The telescopes and some other parts were mailed in from the states. The Army didn't know about them yet.

Other crews looked over the hardware, immediately realizing the guns packed a lot of firepower. No weapons of this type had been seen in Cam Ranh Bay. The men in the club were from different branches of the military, transferring from the south to the north. They had never seen a single-shot 50 caliber with a high-powered scope.

The zappers were bragging about the range and killing power of their hand cannons.

"With these scopes we can actually aim these cannons."

"The range is ten thousand yards."

The gun crews saw an empty table and walked over. Cowboy and Lefty moved their hand cannon onto the table and set it up on its base. Then the crew sat around with the barmaids. They were doing table service and talking to everyone, being very nice to our newbies. It was a good business for the saloon girls. They teased all the new soldiers and sat in their laps. These Madame Butterfly girls showed them lots of attention and much petting. It was like the Wild West: everyone was a hard-core drinker and gunslinger and only the dancehall girls wore silk.

The bar was almost full, and still more were coming in. Then the talk got real and turned to target practice. All the soldiers wanted to prove their skills.

Sergeant Scheffler pipped up. "Only way to really know how good these guns are is to try them out."

Cheers went out all around. They all knew what that meant. Flunky and Steamer grabbed the gun off the table.

Drinks in hand all the sharpshooters with half the people in the bar walked outside to the beer garden, which was also the bathroom, looking for targets. Being nighttime and totally dark, the only targets were the lights over the gates in the harbor. Scheffler wanted to shoot out the lights in the harbor supply area, knowing this would help O'Riley and his men, who were already moving through the buildings and the docks.

The betting started. Scheffler held all the money and the IOUs. All of the riflemen had stacked up sandbags and were waiting for their turn to get off a shot. All the hand cannons were using tracers. Some of the men were using M14s with scopes but were watching the gun truck crews with their hand cannons on the line. Shotgun Eddie was talking with a Navy Seal who wanted to purchase one of his 50-caliber hand cannons. He wanted it for tonight's shooting match and paid upfront.

The Marines also wanted to shoot the hand cannons, to try them out. A target was agreed on. Shoot out the guard tower lights.

We priced the guns from left to right. All the men were amazed at the accuracy of the hand cannon. Everyone with a hand cannon easily took out their target. Most of the men with M14s missed and wanted a second chance and were willing to buy a new weapon. The betting started all over again.

A sharpshooter from the 1st Calvary, who had just bought himself a hand cannon, was very happy with his new toy.

"Damn, this thing is good."

He stood and pulled some items out of his pockets. He wanted to bet some of his personable items. He brought out a dozen human ears, which he had cut off while on patrol in an area called "The Dog's Head" – a two-week search-and-destroy mission. The ears were still flexible.

"I bet a pair a ears I can get that farthest light."

~ MANG YANG PASS ~

Three other soldiers from his unit were now offering up other body parts. "These make great presents. Mail them home to your little brother. He could take them to school for show and tell."

They picked out more lights to shoot out, but the alcohol was adding up for me. I ended up face down, my forehead on a sandbag, a smile on my face. I was feeling no pain.

One by one the soldiers got in their bets and prepared for the next shot. The first Marine shot too low, and Flunky shot too high on his target. Out of the more than a dozen, only five lights remained. They were running out of targets and started looking farther out, toward the ship lights. They all agreed on a target, and with that they moved their sandbags to aim toward the harbor. Bets were all down. They were all shooting hand cannons with red tracers.

Betting again and looking for more targets, they were in position for the next round of targets.

"Last round, boys. Get your bets in," Scheffler called out.

Someone pointed toward the water. "How about a moving target?"

The men turned to a group of fishing boats coming out from the old fishing village farther back in the harbor.

"Agreed," Scheffler said, "Double or nothing."

The old wooden boats were slowly breaking through the waves, heading out for their night's work. The drunken soldiers made their bets. The targets: a moving front and rear light on the same fishing boat. The shooters agreed and got set up on their sandbags. Scheffler collected all the final bets.

Lefty put a wad of cash in Scheffler's hand. "I bet all this and my cannon that I can get both lights."

It was Lefty, Cowboy, Bogard, McNulty, a Navy Seal, and a Marine on the line.

Lefty took his position. He was the first shooter. He hit the front and rear light. The Marine also shot out both lights of his target. Cowboy hit the first light but his second shot to the rear was fired too fast and the boat was moving through the waves with unpredictable motion. He was out.

Bogard hit below the deck lights, starting a small fire. The next was the Navy Seal. He complained about the weapon he just purchased, but he made his bet and shot out both lights, then looked at Schreffler for his payoff. Watching his red tracers, they came to realize a 50-caliber round only had to pass within two feet of the light to blow it out.

For round two the only people to shoot against each other were the dead-eye Marine and McNulty. The Navy Seal and Lefty dropped out. They both had had too much to drink. Each one was hollering and congratulating themselves. Sergeant Scheffler was still fairly sober. He stood up and informed all the shooters about the science of the rifle; the quality of their shooting, the air pressure – called kinetic energy – was the thing that blew out the light. A couple of sharpshooters were nodding their heads yes; they didn't know that.

At the same time everyone looked toward the perimeter of the harbor. The men on guard duty around the harbor had been searching the outside perimeter, looking for movement, thinking the North Vietnamese were firing on them. They located our firing position and turned on searchlights, sending up flares to mark the NCO's position. It was time to give it up. All lights from nearby guard towers were focusing in our direction. All the men quickly headed back inside, Scheffler still holding the money and the IOUs for the last round.

Everyone got very serious about their payments. Then a fight started. The barkeeper called for the shore patrol MPs to break it up. All the Madame Butterflies huddled in the corner to watch. The bartender ran to the end of the bar to grab an AK-47. He pulled it from behind the icemaker and fired two short bursts, then one long burst. He shot a Z-pattern of bullet holes through the tin roof, bringing forty or more light beams in from the beer garden.

Twenty or more shore patrol MPs came in the front door. The MPs were not trying to arrest anyone, only the drunks who couldn't walk and were throwing punches and full beer cans at each other. A sergeant shouted and waved his flashlight. Then he blew his whistle.

"The shore patrol is now in charge. Stand still. No one is leaving. You're all under arrest!"

At this point everyone started running for the back door. McNulty found Chico and threw him over his back, then made tracks. Tiny was staggering around and did the same when he found Ammatwozeo sitting in a chair face down on the table. Burnie and Shotgun Eddie helped each other like two old senior citizens. Sergeant Scheffler ran back and forth, looking for any of the 573 crew. He saw Yogi, who was trying to carry his hand cannon by himself, so Scheffler grabbed one end of the weapon and they ran as best they could for the door. Scheffler grabbed a bottle of Johnny Walker Red on the way out.

The two Navy Seals were right behind them, carrying out a couple of guys they didn't even know. They ran into Jerry Jeff Whitelaw, who carried out as many bottles of alcohol as he could. They helped him out as they passed, each taking one bottle off his hands. The 1st Calvary crew of ten or more left together but first passed behind the bar, gathering up loose bottles, shouting out they were going to bring artillery down on this place.

I opened my eyes, still laying on the sandbags, but I couldn't move. At a full run or doing the best all the men in the bar could, staggering and fast walking, they escaped the shore patrol, most of them running back to the motor pool, off into the darkness. Soldiers were all fully armed and drunk so the MPs didn't take chances; they just followed them.

While all this was going on, O'Riley's people had gathered together again with flashlights and were given their last instructions and maps to take other items on the shopping list. The sun would be up in less than two hours. They were walking and running down the side road, calling to O'Riley's drivers to bring up the forklift and flatbed truck. They had been to the front docks and were taking a different direction out.

Moving into the refrigerated class one yard, the scouts called out, "Everything's a go over here!"

The Navy had too much good stuff to just sit in storage. The troops in the Highland country needed supplies, and at the top of their list was good food and liquor. Their luck had been good all night, and they came upon another big-ticket item. Just before they reached the outer perimeter fence of the shipyard supply base, they came across the power station with three large generators, two of which were shut down. The Korean officer from the Blue Dragon was bidding on each generator and wanted the fuel tank too. Everyone agreed, and they put out the call to bring up a vehicle for loading. They knew the refrigeration units were right next door and they were anxious to load up. They picked out the first generator and started loosening it from its footings. Within minutes they had it loaded onto one of the new OD (olive drab) Green vehicles they had taken. They also decided to load two of the 200-gallon fuel tanks onto the truck, then go back into the power station and disassemble and load the second generator.

The next target was the motor pool utility building, and the band of thieves started loading new tires and rims. Four scouts managed to move an air compressor out to the road and with some help move it onto one of their new trucks. Daylight was just a half hour away, and Sergeant O'Riley's crew made their way out of the supply base without a word. At this point O'Riley was looking for anything of interest that wasn't nailed down. They found a utility building with lots of small generators and three good-sized gasoline-operated welders, very tradeable on the black market. Everything was loaded in twenty minutes.

A Korean soldier found an unattended Jeep and generator on wheels. Some men from the Special Forces had also found it but the South Koreans claimed it for themselves, because they grabbed it first, so they quickly drove it off. Now the flatbed trailer was totally full, so they had to abandon the forklift. Actually, they were giving it back to the Air Force, who they stole it from. They turned their attention to the refrigerated class one yard.

Everyone came running; there were lots of good things to eat. They located a dark area in the fence right behind the reefer. Cutting a hole through the fence, they came across three refrigeration units totally full, a perfect last grab. It was too irresistible, frozen chicken and steaks and hundreds of Easter hams, just for the taking. The morning light was helping them move faster.

Sergeant O'Riley put out the word, "We're going to cut and run."

Doc Murray and his crew drove up in a new truck. He was happy he had scored everything on his want list. And it was a bonus day; they found the liquor, so the entire crew began loading. All the men were running a marathon, making dozens of trips back and forth, loading up treasures, throwing most of the frozen goods in and on top of the flatbed, then the alcohol into the Jeep. When that was full, they used the new truck from Doc Murray's crew, which was now almost fully loaded.

O'Riley came out from around the corner with one of his Special Forces friends. They had dismantled a minigun off a helicopter for their last item. They were looking around for more but they were out of time.

O'Riley put the call out, "Start to rope down the loads and head for the front gate to join the convoy!"

~ JAMES VOELKER ~

The captain was in a meeting till late and spent the night at the officers' quarters. Now he was back with the convoy and making his first call of the day. "Everyone get your boots on; we're moving out in one hour. Time to de de mow."

O'Riley's crew all moved out; they were done looking for anything of value. New trucks were fully loaded from a search out and steal. The flatbed with other trucks moved to the assembly area with all the other 18-wheelers. Many soldiers were walking around but some were fast asleep up in the cargo bay of an 18-wheeler or the gun box of a gun truck and wanted to sleep a little longer. The drivers were warming up the motors. Everyone was more than anxious to get out of the area before things got ugly. O'Riley's crew was mixed in with the rest of the trucks. They parked themselves in between two tankers and another flatbed 18-wheeler so no one could see them. The 573 had been kicked out of the Da Nang supply base before for this kind of behavior. They were only allowed on base with a Marine escort and orders for everything – no SOS.

Radio talk was starting to come on with wake-up calls. Crews took down their hammocks and started to load up. They noticed that half of their hand cannons were missing. Some of them were still feeling no pain, while others, like me, had fairly large headaches. It was time to roll.

Security police talk was coming in. They had a very good idea who was to blame for everything that happened last night. On the field radios there was no communications coming from the convoy; the crews knew to keep quiet. Scheffler was calling out the F word, calling everybody names. It was time to do the road. Most of us wouldn't eat anything until the first pitstop. Some would eat breakfast out of a can onboard their truck.

Captain Shorts climbed into the Batmobile. Scheffler already had the motor running.

~ MANG YANG PASS ~

Captain Shorts puts out a call, "Time to de de mow.

"Everything go as planned; did I get my mini gun? Anyone see O'Riley this morning? We can't leave without him and his crew."

Scheffler put the call out, "You in line for the convoy, O'Riley?"

O'Riley immediately called back. "I want to leave right now. Go ahead."

The captain was getting suspicious, he looked over at Scheffler and said one word, "Well?"

A call was coming in on the field radio from the Navy Shore Patrol. They wanted to talk to Captain Shorts and question some of his men about the multiple problems from last evening.

"We've already moved out," he said, then looked over at Scheffler and gave him a dirty smile.

"I don't want to know. We're not going to count heads here. Tell everyone to move out."

Scheffler immediately called out to all his gun trucks, shouting, "Wind 'em up. Read my lips, you mother truckers. Better be ready. Bring all firepower to the front. Move out double shoulder. If the gate isn't open, we'll blow it open."

He didn't have to repeat the order.

Scheffler added, "Find Sergeant O'Riley and take all of his raiding party with you. We'll meet up at Mamason's bakery at the third turn out. De de mow now, I mean now. All lights on. Don't stop for anything. Do the road, pronto!"

The Batmobile was speeding toward the harbor side gate, driving past his gun truck crews, which were all lined up side-by-side. Captain Shorts stood up on his seat and gave the signal to move out. He counted four gun trucks storming out; two were still in the motor pool. The SS Alabama was waiting for Instant Hell, which didn't want to start. Chico came up behind him and got on the radio to Lefty. Time for a push. Going bumper to bumper, Chico gave a gentle push to start the old vehicle.

Bogard told the SS Alabama, "You know the routine; count to ten then back off."

It worked the very first time. A cloud of black smoke came out of the exhaust pipe.

In one minute we were all on the move, taking up the entire road. The gun trucks were all moving next to each other for the exit gate and the open road. It was a game to see who would give up and drop back. They only had a couple of hundred yards to decide before leaving for the side gate.

The entire convoy gave the traveling signal. O'Riley was one of the first flatbeds to move out. Captain Shorts fired off his flare gun. They didn't want to wait around to talk to the Navy Shore Patrol. Five trucks, then ten trucks, then ten more behind them, another five more in motion within minutes. All the trucks were moving out at almost full speed.

Half a dozen blue shore patrol jeeps were moving up and down the line of trucks, trying to get someone's attention to stop. Flipping off the shore patrol with a goodbye of one finger and two words, no one gave them a second look. Several shore patrol jeeps kept following the convoy, even after it moved off from the base. The SS Alabama and Instant Hell were bringing up the rear. It was a perfect exit. All of the trucks of the convoy had moved out in less than five minutes.

The shore patrol didn't want to give up the chase. Speeding up, two jeeps, one on each side of the front vehicle, were unable to pull Instant Hell over, so they dropped back behind the SS Alabama, with another shore patrol Jeep driving side-by-side; the three were determined to keep up the chase. In the passenger seat the Sergeant of the guard was standing up, shouting and waving a 45. Pulling up closer behind the SS Alabama, shining their headlights, they shouted something about being the law here and for them to stop.

The gun truck crew in the cargo bay all agreed to take a

bathroom break off the rear of the truck and with a small amount of effort were able to hit the windshield. After that they spun the 106 and the 105 around and pointed the barrels down at the driver of the shore patrol, then put three flashlights down the barrel, shining the light in the driver's eyes. At this point the shore patrol gave up but put out a radio call to their fellow SPs to cut off the convoy, but no one showed.

Instant Hell brought down the whip antennas and tied on a flashlight and a green flag. All the other gun trucks did the same. The field radios were talking back and forth. Even O'Riley was giving out his congratulations. Everyone was anxious to put some miles on and leave Cam Ranh Bay behind them. As daylight broke, the convoy was moving at a normal speed, enjoying the sunrise and fresh air.

CHAPTER 11

*T*wo hours down the road we were coming up to Mamason's bakery so we slowed down.

The men requested a breakfast break and Captain Shorts agreed to a one-hour layover. He told all the radiomen to bring down their antennas and send up the red flag. We had a long day in front of us. Seeing her small village come up, we pulled over. Mamason knew we were coming, and their family already had rice bread out drying in the sun. This small roadside bread shop was everybody's favorite stop. One of her specialties was duck eggs with fried rice and onions. Several Madame Butterflies lived in the building next door. We stopped here almost every time. There was no sign-up. They didn't need one. Everyone called the place Mamason's bakery.

~ MANG YANG PASS ~

Sergeant O'Riley always got whatever he wanted for free. She had a very nice icemaker and generator, which she got from the black market. Mamason herself was more than likely a middleman of the black market. She had a great smile. Her teeth were all shiny black from chewing opium nuts.

O'Riley was on the radio to Tony Lee, who was driving one of the new trucks they just acquired. It was almost fully loaded down with some medical supplies for Doc Murray along with other tools and a half dozen air-conditioners. They gave the hand signal to pullover right in front of the bakery. The other flatbeds pulled over on both sides of the road. Captain Shorts was waiting for O'Riley. He wanted his first look at the mini gun. The entire convoy had pulled off. Men were walking from truck to truck and over to the bakery to get a cold soda and something to eat.

Everyone gathered around and started bragging. O'Riley and his men divided up the steaks and hams to all the crews, among other mouthwatering treats. It was the best way to say thank you from him and his crew. O'Riley knew very well what the 573 gun truck crews would do that night, which made a perfect diversion for him. He sold off some food and a few things to Mamason and her family and then walked back to his Jeep with Scheffler.

The Batmobile sent up a flare, and everyone ran back to their trucks. The freight train on wheels was heading back into the Highland Mountains. We would not call the helicopters for support until we reached the slow-going, winding road five hours away.

We were coming out of the Delta, rice paddies on both sides of the road, and moving into the foothills before grinding our way into the mountains. With the night behind us, the fresh air and moving vehicles felt good. Everyone hoped we would get away with what we had done in Cam Ranh Bay. Like little kids, we didn't think anyone could prove what went on, and we didn't start the fight. The fully loaded flatbed truck drivers had double checked their loads at Mamason's. After this point we were entering Hell's door: bad roads. Going up was the same as coming down; you had to prepare for a firefight, but going back up, we were weighed down with supplies. It was very slow going. The convoy cruised along, avoiding all the potholes, which meant slowing down even more and moving from right to left.

We could see the hilltops coming up, the road leading back home. Captain Shorts was in the lead. He got on the radio and requested we bring up the green flags and the American flag. Everything was green to go. He hadn't said a word about the bar fight. We would deal with that back in Pleiku.

The convoy had not only picked up all needed supplies for dozens of camps and outposts. We had an assortment of new men, most all on their first tour. They were new soldiers right from the states, only been in the Army six months. This was their first look at being in the field. Some had been waiting to get into a fight and serve. Others disliked what they saw and began talking with each other about being reassigned. They had heard a lot of bad things about the Central Highlands. One of the newbies asked about a bowling team he wanted to be on and should he have brought his own bowling ball. He was riding in the back of Ground Pounder,

Flunky nicely explained, "The only game we play is horseshoes with hand grenades."

The newbie's face went blank. His eyes opened up and his mouth closed.

Flunky continued. "The Army is on the attack, something big. More than likely another push over the border. Two Core is on the move. Battalion headquarters is bringing in troops. All you new people are in for your first long walk in the Highlands."

We were anticipating another push into Bullet Hole Woods from the Highlands, an operation we were doing once every three to six months. Special forces had at least ten new personnel; all were officers. With tiger-striped special jungle fatigues, we knew they were up to something.

The new people looked at one another. Three or four of them began talking about re-enlistment to get out of going into Cambodia, which meant these soldiers had to re-enlist for two more years or more to get out of Vietnam. They wanted to call their congressman and talk to a priest. They wanted to be re-assigned to Germany. Some men came for this action and wanted to serve for the experience. They would become gunners and second drivers after one or two road trips up and down Mang Yang Pass, giving them time to learn all the turns.

Instant Hell had picked up one driver and a gunner. Ground Pounder had three new men who were up for the duty. One new guy told the story about being a second-generation soldier. Iron Butterfly had two new members, both shipped in from Fort Hood Texas. One from Mission, Texas, a young Hispanic. He said his family and friends all called him The Cisco Kid. His real name was Dickie. The Cisco Kid told everybody he was a border rat. Back home he would go back and forth over the border almost every day just to buy and sell whatever people wanted. But now Dickie said he had been waiting for his chance to serve in the field. He had sniper training and wanted to be on point. He had never heard of gun trucks but liked what he saw and wanted to try the hand cannon.

Dickie said, "Everyone back home wants me to write and tell about my great adventures."

I piped up. "When we reach the 573, I'll take you to the dug-out, our armory, and show you the gun shop and assembly table." Then I smiled. "We're a little short on hand cannons right now. We had one hell of a bad night."

The other guy's nickname was Breeze. He laughed and added, "When you fell asleep on the sandbags, you missed the best part of the evening." Breeze started talking about the bar fight and the shore patrol telling everyone to stop. "It was just like being back home in LA."

Breeze opened his wallet and showed us a photograph of himself. "Here's me and my bike."

He was wearing his biker patches and his hair cut high and tight, squared-off, and a full beard. He looked like the guy from the Old Testament. He was standing in front of a line of choppers with forty of his brother bikers. He ran a three-wheeled Harley-Davidson with all secondhand parts. The nickname from his club fit him perfectly; Breeze was a talking head, and he was a smooth talker, too. He also knew when to listen. He would make a good used car salesman but wanted to become some type of legal advisor when he got home.

At Mamasans earlier that day Flunky looked him over. He thought he was just another kid; an automatic distrust had begun. They were from two different biker clubs. The only thing they had in common was they got biker tattoos at the same Tijuana shop.

All the trucks were gearing down to start their climb back up into the mountains. Captain Shorts was with Ground Pounder, traveling down the left side of the convoy, watching to see if everybody was ready and up for the challenge. They turned and went back to the front again, looking for O'Riley. Shorts wanted to keep track of his mini gun. O'Riley had moved to the back of the brand-new truck and was talking with his Special Forces friends.

As they moved along, the gun truck radios were calling in, bragging up their shooting. Lefty and Bogard bragged about being the last man standing, pointing their fingers and blaming everyone else but themselves.

The convoy was winding its way through the half-dozen hairpin turns. Their fully loaded vehicles were showing their age. They had to downshift while going through the first turn.

~ MANG YANG PASS ~

Jerry Jeff was on the field radio with Sergeant Scheffler, wanting to know the location of O'Riley. Everyone was interested in his buying and selling business.

Just barely moving along, making the road's steep upgrade and bad turns, there was still four more hours of slow road. Special forces had loaded some equipment into one of the brand-new two-and-a-half-ton trucks with absolutely no identification. The captain pulled up alongside O'Riley's truck. Usually, Captain Shorts barely gave O'Riley a look, but now he had his Gatling gun, his mini gun, in the back of his vehicle. Captain Shorts saluted and kept moving. Everyone with O'Riley saluted back. O'Riley got on the field radio with the Batmobile. "Heard anything good or bad from the shore patrol?"

"I haven't heard a thing. It's quiet and that's good," Shorts replied.

The shore patrol didn't want to come into the Central Highlands. And it could take them a week to figure out what we had done.

The 573 was happy to get some new personnel. One of the newbies was a Sergeant. He re-enlisted to come back to the Highlands. He was sick of the stateside "Girl Scouts," the officers who would give him grief about the littlest regulation infractions. Someone told him about another "search out and destroy" into Bullet Hole Woods.

As the day wore on, the convoy slowly wound its way up Mang Yang Pass. All the trucks were loaded to the max but we still made good time.

Captain Shorts got on the radio. "Chico, how far are we spread out?"

"We've moving with two truck lengths in-between each vehicle," he responded.

This was what the North Vietnamese were waiting for, the

next eighty miles up the hill, slow road, and good targets. A perfect trap.

Small arms fire started coming in. Groups of NVA snipers were aiming for the drivers. The snipers were well hidden, impossible to see, hundreds of feet above the road.

Captain Shorts got on the horn. "We need helicopter support! Put some snakes in the air!"

A half-hour later he called back again, this time to the Air Force or Army. "Give me some air support, anything you've got, damn it! Give me a Cobra gunship. Put some snakes in the air!"

We were coming up to the worst miles of the pass. Every mile we drove up the pass we were moving into the Viet Cong's home territory. Every mile brought more gunfire down on us.

Shorts heard a reply. "Bad news. You got to get out of that place immediately. There will be no helicopter support of any kind.

"Nothing good is coming up. The ground and air are going to be too dangerous. Get your helmets on and get down and kiss your behind goodbye. Hell is coming from the sky."

The walkie-talkie went silent. Captain Shorts heard the last from air command.

"Damn it! Get me Two Core. He tried to reach Two Core and Brigade Field Command. No one told him about the airstrike. He was no longer talking; he was screaming and calling for the bombing to be stopped.

The convoy was just entering the road called Thirteen Curves; the road was uphill hairpins and switchbacks. The last of the convoy's trucks were just entering Thirteen Curves. Halfway through, the lead vehicles were starting into the worst turn, all with fully overloaded vehicles.

He called back, "Speed up. We've got to make better time!"

Most everything we were transporting was explosive.

Chico and Tiny were on the field radio to Captain Shorts. "Should we break formation and give the big rigs a push?"

~ MANG YANG PASS ~

Lefty and McNulty were listening in. "Good idea!"

Captain Shorts agreed. He was back on the radio with all gun trucks as they prepared for new orders. The gun trucks were taking on fire and returning fire.

Several crews piped up, "Where's our air support? We need some helicopter support."

Captain Shorts sent out the bad news, "No air support; the choppers aren't coming."

Many tankers were overloaded with JP4 jet fuel and other fuels. Others were fully loaded with artillery shells. All were calling, wanting a good explanation.

Captain Shorts replied within minutes, "The Air Force based out of Takhli, Thailand is going to hit us on both sides with a Bs airstrike." (A B-52 airstrike.)

The Air Force was using the convoy to draw in the NVA but failed to tell Captain Shorts. Hearing this, everyone watched the sky behind them, looking for bombers. The call went back to all the other trucks, "We've got Bs coming."

We still had to watch the road. A small reflection was seen behind us in the far-off distance, white lines in the sky. Maybe forty-five minutes or less before we became a target, a drop zone. We called a B-52 strike "rolling thunder." It was a forest fire and earthquake all in one, and it was bearing down on us. Supposedly targeting the hilltops and Ia Drang Valley, on both sides of the pass, but we could easily get in the way.

Captain Shorts radioed to all the gun trucks, "Break formation. Move to the lead vehicles and get behind the green elephants. Push the big rigs over the last hill, through the pass."

Whiskey Train and Iron Butterfly in the very front received their new orders, breaking off from the convoy and doing a fast U-turn, immediately moving in behind the first two overloaded 18-wheelers. We usually only did this bumper-to-bumper push in the rainy season. We got in position and started to push two flatbeds loaded down with artillery shells.

The other gun trucks were coming up at full speed almost crashing into the 18-wheelers, then downshifting, throwing caution to the wind, lining up on the next four 18-wheelers. Bogard and Ammatwozeo got on the radio to tell the 18-wheelers to spread out so each gun truck could get in-between and push them. Instant Hell and Ground Pounder were bumper-to-bumper, pushing overloaded vehicles. Big Daddy Virgo Rat was not far behind. Whiskey Train was already grinding its tires, tearing up the road while giving a push to the first vehicle. Crews on all gun trucks were still watching the sky.

Someone shouted out, "I see more white lines in the sky, ten maybe fifteen, straight behind us!"

All the gun truck crews were picking up the pace, calling to one another, "Do the road!" It was a rally call.

At full speed they were bouncing around and weaving in and out and around boulders, knocking down the brush and small trees. The S.S. Alabama came back down and hit several boulders and slid up against a fuel tanker, sliding and scraping the length of the truck. Big Daddy Virgo Rat came back down for its second push. Driving fully off the road almost at full speed, the truck ran over a large flat stone and for several seconds the entire gun truck was airborne. Hitting down on its front tires, everybody in the gun box was thrown forward.

Cowboy stood up to look over the side. It was straight down. He wished he had a parachute. Ammatwozeo regained control and kept moving. He reached the place in the road where it was wide enough to accommodate a turnaround. A small stream of water was coming down, making it muddy but just enough to do a very fast U-turn, keeping their speed up but downshifting to increase power. Cowboy got on the headphones in the cargo bay, shouting to Ammatwozeo, "I'm going to pour in a gallon of JP4. We need the power now!"

Pouring it in slowly, the motor began to sound like a jet. He shifted up one gear but kept his foot on the accelerator. Sliding sideways, they powered across the stream.

It looked like a boat race. With the Iron Butterfly right behind them, they barely missed each other as they passed. Steamer was on the radio to all the flatbed crews to be prepared. Everybody on the Iron Butterfly held onto the sides of the truck, with their heads and shoulders jerking back and forth. The transmission and drivetrain of the truck sounded like a sledgehammer squeezing against a hard surface.

In the cargo bay of Iron Butterfly, Steamer added JP4 jet fuel into our fuel line. Instant Hell had come back down and started their second push, squeezing their way in-between a fully loaded tanker that was falling behind, slowing down the convoy. Everyone still watched dozens of white lines coming their way. Two more big rigs were being pushed to the hilltop, bumpers bound together, grinding the old vehicles for everything they had. Lefty talked to his truck as if it was his girlfriend on date night. There was loose gravel dust in the air mixed with the smell of boiling transmission fluid. Instant Hell slid to the right then the left toward the edge of the road. The smell of rubber and diesel fuel was everywhere. There was no guardrail out there, only the cliff. Nothing but the air. They repositioned themselves, back to the center and shifted to another gear. They increased their speed to get the tankers up over the next hill.

They looked up and saw the light reflecting off the planes with white lines in the sky coming closer. We still had a little time but not much. The trucks were climbing out of the hairpin, the grade of the highway increased. The gun trucks were still being held back by the fully loaded vehicles.

On their walkie-talkies, the faster and lighter gun trucks were shouting four-letter words and saying, "We're all leaving together, making it to the top!"

The drivers of the gun trucks were tempted to keep going and not go back but the words "We all go down together" were in their blood. It was part of their code. There were no second thoughts, so all turned around and started back down, almost at full speed.

As the four gun trucks passed the last 18-wheelers, they did a fast U-turn and power-slid into the side of a hill, dirt and stones falling into the gun box. The trucks came close to the edge with their front tires and almost went over. The gun trucks scraped each other while getting back in line for another push, shifting gears, slamming the cargo and the men back and forth. It's only a matter of minutes and they would be buried alive. The NVA were up above us, enjoying our problem.

The lines in the sky were minutes from being overhead. Then it started. The B-52 bombers dropped their payload on the ridge a mile behind. Another line of bombs dropped in the valley, coming our way. Rolling thunder was death from the sky and it was coming from the right and left with the 573 in the middle, the flashpoint getting closer. The hot day just got hotter.

Chapter 12

The North Vietnamese were no longer shooting but the convoy had a long way to reach flat road and safety. The Airforce was dropping 500-pound bombs, a dozen at a time, targeting the back side of the ridge. Napalm was also being dropped farther behind, down the middle and side of the huge valley, on the other side of the ridgetop, and down into the canyon. One-hundred-foot-tall flames and explosions were coming down. The head of the convoy got clear, but not for long. All one could do was hold on; the air itself was being sucked up.

There was no hiding place. The Air Force was hoping to hit and wipe out the retreating NVA unit. One of the gun truck drivers, we don't know who, was screaming out in pain. It sounded like Jerry Jeff.

"Man oh man, I hit my head and shoulders on the roof over that last bump and came down on my private parts. I gave myself a hernia! I crushed my crotch. I need a doctor, or a nurse might be better!"

That's what happened when only wearing a pair of boxers for your uniform.

The convoy was covered in rolling smoke, and the ground was shaking. It was impossible to count how many trucks were still down in what was left of the road, working their way through the last bad turns, then the last mile, which was an uphill grade.

~ JAMES VOELKER ~

The firestorm was coming our way fast. Everyone could feel the heat and shockwave. You didn't have to look in your mirror; you just had to look right or left or straight up. If you were not holding onto something, you'd be thrown over the side from the shock wave of the explosions.

Entire trees were flying through the air, completely engulfed in flames. The bombs had been dropped within a couple hundred yards above and below the trucks on both sides, the shockwave blowing the fully loaded 18-wheelers from one side of the road and then another explosion pushing the vehicle back. In a matter of minutes we would reach the plateau, a straightaway that would give the convoy a getaway.

A voice came over the squawk box, "Stay in control. Don't break formation; it won't do any good to try and pass up the slower ones."

The SS Alabama had already pushed two cargo trucks to the top and returned down to the next heavily loaded 18-wheeler.

Tiny, from the SS Alabama, called out, "We're in trouble! The napalm fire caught up to us. Don't think we can hold out. Send the next gun truck to drop back and pick us up!"

We lost count of the vehicles. All the gun trucks were still pushing vehicles. We knew there was still more down there in the hairpin turns. The airstrike was on both sides of the road the whole length of the convoy. The high cliffs created an updraft, giving the drivers a view of the road. The sky was getting black, blocking off the sun. The thick air was partially filling our lungs with smoke. Luckily, there was a strong wind that was pushing the firestorm over the hilltop.

Just when everyone thought they were going to be burned alive, the bombing stopped. Drivers still had a long way to go, and they were looking around for the rest of their crews. Things begin to ease up; the shaking from side to side stopped. The firestorm was still coming at us from behind, a draft of wind moving faster, swallowing and bounding up the hillside. You couldn't see anything behind and only a hundred feet ahead. The vehicles were all spread out but we kept moving.

Captain Shorts yelled over the radio, "There will be no one left behind. All vehicles keep rolling!"

Several large napalm strikes were blowing up the hilltop. A third push of gun trucks and 18-wheelers was coming out of the smoke, reaching the end of the drop zone. The firestorm was over ten miles long on both sides of the road. The 18-wheelers reached the safety of the straightaway. The B-52s moved off and out of sight. The firestorm was still blazing but it looked as if we were going to make it. One by one the tankers were being pushed up with help. For the fourth time, gun trucks headed back down into the smoke-filled roadside. Coming down through the smoke and fire, the gun trucks found their next set of flatbeds and reefer trucks. It was O'Riley's crew. They were so overloaded the vehicles were in danger of being caught up in the fire.

As they were being pushed out, the gun trucks wanted a headcount, so they knew if there was anyone behind them, but they couldn't make an accurate count of the vehicles that were out of the drop zone.

Chico was on the field radio with bad news, "We're burnt too bad; we can't go any farther."

Smoking Joe and Tiny yelled out, "Abandon ship!"

The crew jumped out and started running up the road. They got picked up by us and Instant Hell. Chico dropped a phosphorus grenade down the barrel of the howitzers then jumped off. Later the captain would order out a tank retriever to bring this vehicle out.

The wind was picking up a little more, helping with an updraft, giving the drivers short views of the road. But more smoke poured out of the valley, which now had a reddish-orange glow from napalm. It made you think you had just died and gained entrance into hell. Above the road, the firestorm closed in.

Hopefully, these were the last of the big rigs coming out of the smoking fog. There were forest fires in the valley and on the hilltop. Both sides were burnt up. Nothing could be alive in that fire.

Then we got a call from Captain Shorts. "There's still five trucks in the hairpin. It's your call. I can't make you go down there."

Three of the radiomen yelled out, "We all go down together!"

Instant Hell and Ground Pounder had turned around and were in line with Iron Butterfly and Big Daddy Virgo Rat, who was already waiting and revving up his motor. Whiskey Train turned around and was bringing up the rear guard. Iron Butterfly was not waiting. Jerry Jeff and I shouted to the other drivers, "We leave now!"

I fired a flair gun straight up. Jerry Jeff revving up the motor then dumped the clutch to move out. I got on the squawk box and shouted to the other gun trucks, "Those are our brothers down there. What the hell are you waiting for?!"

That's all it took; all the gun trucks took off. We were told on the field radio to keep a straight line.

The road to get back there was a firestorm. We knew if the 18-wheelers and tankers were in one of the hairpin turns, they could not transmit but we kept trying. A gun truck flare went straight up; we were hoping to get a recognition signal. We were moving slow. Visibility had increased slightly. Two miles or more down the road we fired another flare. This time we got a response not far down the road. One flare could be seen above the smoke within a minute. Another two flares were visible, then another one. There were five trucks not far in front of us.

The radio came alive with laughs and howling. Everyone was calling in. We told the convoy drivers to spread out as they came out of the last hairpin turn, cutting their way through the smoke.

~ MANG YANG PASS ~

All the gun trucks did a fast U-turn and moved into position for a push. Iron Butterfly was one of the first to give a starting push. I got on the radio to Jerry Jeff, "It's time to head for home."

Ground Pounder and Big Daddy Virgo Rat fell into place and started to push tankers filled with diesel fuel. If just one of them blew up, there wouldn't be anything left; it would take out all the other trucks and we would all be cremated.

Instant Hell and Iron Butterfly were coming up through the smoke and fire, behind two overloaded flatbeds that were hauling 175 artillery shells. All the shells were facing to the back, which meant they were facing the gun truck drivers. In front of them was approximately three miles of firestorm to push through, flames coming across the road.

For the first time in hours the radios were dead silent. All men knew what they volunteered for. The life expectancy of a convoy crew member was only four months. All these men had lived longer than that; they were overdue. For the next forty-five minutes all we could do was keep our minds on the road.

A call came in from Captain Shorts. "Give us a sign."

With that half a dozen flares were fired off from the convoy.

Captain Shorts immediately replied, "You're going to make it!"

The radio stayed silent as the convoy drivers saw green hilltops through the wind and smoke. They were only a couple hundred yards to the hilltop.

"I need a damage report and headcount," Captain Shorts radioed.

With a very dry mouth Smoking Joe called for a roll call.

Coming to the crest of the hill, they rejoined their unit, which was spread out over a couple miles. Everyone was all smiles; they just dodged two dozen B-52s bombs, and behind them was nothing more than smoldering ashes. All one could do now was wait for the green flag order.

~ JAMES VOELKER ~

An old push-pull Cessna aircraft dropped down to 400 feet. The copilot was taking pictures. This plane was the forward spotter for the B-52s. The bird dog was low enough to see us watching and five minutes later the pilot turned around and came back overhead to drop down even closer. The pilot and copilot were on the radio.

"Arne and Mitch here. Congrats, gentlemen, for making it out alive! We've got it all on film. You're going to be famous! This is Hawkeye Still Photography saying adios."

They were proud of what they did to us.

This was the plane that called in the airstrike. The old push-pull prop job did a victory rollover just in front of the killing field. The gun truck crews knew this was the plane that almost killed them all.

Multiple requests were heard. "Captain, request permission to shoot that SOB out of the sky."

"Request denied," came Short's quick reply, "But when they come back, I think a few tracers directly in front of them might be in order."

When the plane came around again, all five gun trucks opened up with tracers one hundred yards ahead of the Cessna.

The pilot immediately broke off. He got the general idea.

We found out later that the airstrike was ordered by Saigon Air Command. There was something big going on. Field command reported strong troop movements in the Highlands. The North Vietnamese all moved for an offensive, which was coming out of Cambodia with new fresh troops. As always, the push was coming through the Ho Chi Minh Trail. The big brass commander didn't tell Captain Shorts or the other ten officers in our convoy who were in headquarters last night. They didn't think we needed to know our fate and didn't want anybody backing out. Captain Shorts' blood was up. He wanted to kill someone back at headquarters. None of the stuffed shirts mentioned the airstrike.

∽

A call came in that a tank retriever was coming out for the SS Alabama. They called for directions. The other gun truck crews were doing their best to forget about what just happened. They put the fires out on all the tires and did a headcount. Overall, most of the trucks needed a new coat of paint on both sides, but we were all up and running, back on the road. In two hours we would be in the homestretch, the bad road behind us.

Chapter 13

Back in the Highlands and on the last set of turns, we started to reorganize home. Captain Shorts asked for volunteers to go back and help retrieve the Alabama. All five crew members from the SS Alabama jumped off the gun trucks they were on. They wanted to see their vehicle for the last time. They wanted to bring it back or what was left of it. They saw the tank retriever and flagged down the oversized monster. Chico, Smoking Joe, Tiny, and two other gunners quickly climbed on the back, holding onto the chains that they would use to pull the SS Alabama. When the tank retriever asked for directions, Chico told him, "It's easy to find; just drive into a wall of fire."

The truck was about fifteen miles back through some heavy smoke from fires still burning. The wind was still blowing everything back up the hill but the burning heat and firestorm had diminished in the past two hours. When they finally reached the SS Alabama, they didn't know if there was anything they could save off the old truck, but they still had to bring the truck back. Quickly attaching chains to the front bumper, they moved out, heading back to the 573.

The convoy had continued and was coming up to the outlying village, going over the first bridge that led into the outer villages and fields of Pleiku. We came across a second bridge where we began to see landmarks. Sandbag Point to the left – a flat sand deposit landmark where people often gathered – and a mile later, Wade Davis Marine Corps base. There was a call for all trucks to turn off. The next turnoff was the South Vietnamese Special Forces base and Two Core headquarters. Across from Two Core on the north side of the road was the VC prison, also known as Crowbar Hotel. It looked like someplace out of the Middle Ages with three continuous rolls of barbed wire and unseen landmines.

At this point the road became very busy with civilians and military personnel traffic.

It was time for some fun. All the heavily loaded trucks were signaling to each other to get ready for their turn. They planned on making it at almost full speed, so they all dropped down one gear and brought the right side of their vehicles carefully off the road and onto a dusty walking path almost level with the blacktop. The drivers were aiming for a dozen prisoner cells, which were lined up on both sides of the main gate. It was solitary confinement for especially dangerous North Vietnamese and Viet Cong prisoners, also called Viet Minh. These cells, called bird cages, were outside the prison and were well-constructed chicken coops just big enough to hold one person. The prisoners were exposed to the weather. The South Korean Rock Army and the South Vietnamese were always on guard in towers and on foot patrol in front of Two Core, right across the street. POWs who were dangerous were punished harshly. Violent breakouts were common and watching inmates constantly was an all-day responsibility.

To keep control of the POWs, these little cells were placed along the road with no roof, only food and water. They were out in the sun all day. People walking by dropped food and cigarettes to them; some were possibly family.

The entire convoy crew was on edge; their blood was up. Captain Shorts got on the field radio and ordered the checkered flag to be sent up (end of the mission) and asked everyone to report their given positions.

Scheffler kept his Jeep on the blacktop. All other trucks that were fully loaded had their own plan. Like a train on a railroad track, aiming for the line of VC bird cages. They intended to scrape the cells with their tires, which gave them the feeling of payback. The entire convoy had come off the road and was bearing down directly on the cells a hundred yards away. Men in the cargo bays were holding on and watching. The radioman topside in each truck was giving details to the driver because he couldn't see past the truck in front of him. The VC watched a storm cloud of red dust coming in with only tires and headlights closing in.

You could hear the gravel crunching as the trucks were accelerating and not much more. The Viet Cong prisoners started to kick their cell doors. They were in for the scare of their lives. Two or three of the big rigs took out the front half of a couple bird cages. Others flattened the front side of the wire cage with tires and bumpers. Some came within only inches of the cells as the trucks moved through civilians and guards, who all moved back or ran way. The last of the convoy passed by the cells and left some very scared Viet Cong.

This was not the first time this had happened, so the Korean guards knew to stay back. Believe it or not, no North Vietnamese were hurt, but they were all quite scared. After what had happened on this trip, there were no regrets on our side. One by one each Army truck took a left turn.

Shorts and Scheffler were on the field radio talking over the deal with Sergeant O'Riley. They wanted to meet up outside the motor pool. This would be the gathering point tonight for all personnel coming into the camp. It was Saturday night, and everyone was looking forward to the evening.

O'Riley's three trucks were directly behind the Batmobile. O'Riley was talking to his new people about the Saturday night campfire and cookout. He suggested parking their trucks off to the side of the center gathering point, which tonight would become the location for Saturday night relaxation. O'Riley signed off. His last words were "Steaks and chicken on me!"

The convoy continued down the last few miles of straightaway, they came to a turnoff called "The Shortcut." A half dozen flatbeds broke off. The Iron Butterfly and Whiskey Train also made the turn and a minute later Instant Hell turned off with five other 18-wheelers.

Military trucks and jeeps were coming and going. It was a steady flow of traffic in both directions, a very busy road. Some were motor-scooter taxis and three-wheeled scooters. The shortcut went around and behind a large hill and over a large stream, making it a good couple miles longer. This very busy road's only purpose was a long line of businesses on both sides of the road. It was the red-light district. Privacy wooden fences, banana trees, taxi service signs, and fishponds were the norm. Some looked like Western-style saloon shacks, and some of the houses displayed names and numbers. This street didn't have any electricity.

Steamer was driving a flatbed now and it was moving slowly, pointing out places of interest, as if being a tour guide to his new friend, Breeze. They admired the "landscape" as the ladies of the evening jumped on the running boards and handed out kisses. Steamer was talking to Breeze, telling him all about the road conditions and the details of his new job. He was giving his new driver his first "personnel" training lesson.

Looking forward to the night off, he needed someone to drive the fully loaded flatbed. Only a minute away was his crib and his girlfriend, Tue. Steamer had been on long patrol before the supply run and hadn't seen Tue for three-and-a-half weeks. He quickly went over the old vehicle's problems with the loose steering wheel, and in a hundred words or less Breeze received his dos and don'ts.

~ JAMES VOELKER ~

(Tue)

"The overloaded truck wants to move to the right. The steering wheel's maybe missing some teeth in the gang box. And it has very little to no breaks."

Breeze nodded yes, taking it all in in a two-minute crash course. Steamer called out, "Just follow all the other trucks and you'll be fine!" His famous last words.

"I guarantee you some hitchhikers will be joining you. Someone will be jumping on, heading for the 573 base camp." Which Breeze had never been to. "Just turn left. This road dead-ends into the 573. You're only hauling explosives; what could happen?"

Then Steamer gave him a big smile, opened the driver's door, and bailed out. Breeze, being a newbie, had a question or two, but when he looked over, he only saw the driver door swinging back and forth and an unmanned steering wheel. He looked out the window and was taken in by the sight of so many ladies of the evening. He moved over to the driver's side. Breeze just became the driver.

Looking out the windshield, there was heavy foot traffic.

~ MANG YANG PASS ~

Some Army and Air Force soldiers were walking on the boardwalk from brothel to brothel with a lady on their arm. Vehicles of all types were coming and going in both directions, some stopping and dropping off ladies and taking photographs on the boardwalk. There were topless young ladies holding up cans of beer and waving what looked like colored handkerchiefs. Their AM radio was playing dance music. They shouted out in broken English, "You all come back now!" The young ladies did another dance and smiled.

Steamer ran into Tue's house where she lived with her two sisters and extended family. Shotgun Eddie and I were already sitting on plastic mats on the ground inside Tue's house. Minutes later Richard and Bogard walked in carrying packages of rice bread, two bottles of bourbon, and one bottle of brandy. They would spend the rest of the day in the back of the tin house called the Palace, underneath the banana trees around the fishpond, watching the silkworms grazing in the bushes. Silkworms were a cash crop for all people in this area.

Tue and Steamer were making plans to be married in the next month and had started the paperwork to have Tue brought back to the states. She already spoke English pretty well and had worked for the French. She knew what was going on in the countryside. Her younger brother and father seemed to know many things about the troop movement, but the men always told their sisters not to talk about their business partners, not wanting the women to be put in harm's way. Tue's family owned a small motorcycle shop and all had lived in Pleiku all their lives. Many of the men were soldiers of fortune and were working on both sides just to stay alive.

Tue told Yogi and me, and some others who also just came in, "There are many enemy forces in the area. They are up in the mountains but intend to move tonight. You're safe for now, but some of you must leave before nightfall." She put her hand on Steamer's shoulder. "But come back in the daytime when it's safe," she says with a smile.

By telling the Americans what she knew, Tue could be putting herself in trouble with the Viet Cong. Steamer and his friends agreed to leave before nightfall. Then he walked out the back door and lay down in a hammock. Tue went to him and asked if he wanted something to eat or drink and offered to relax him with a back walk.

They talked for a while, and Tue's small children brought them each a bowl of rice. They moved and sat by a small cooking stove where Tue's sister was frying up some chicken and duck. Shotgun Eddie and I and some children walked back to the cook stove with a frying pan. We had enough for everyone, sharing some of the good loot from Sergeant O'Riley.

On the road, Breeze's flatbed was slowly moving along but didn't stop, as many soldiers were walking along the side of the road. A person jumped onto the pile of artillery shells and sat with four other men. Breeze leaned out of the window and called out, "Where to? No smoking!"

They all replied, "The 573. It's fight night!"

Minutes later, four more men jumped onto the running board and give a friendly greeting. Within ten seconds another GI ran up alongside and jumped onto the running board. Breeze slowly drove past several dozen brothels, which were on both sides of the road. The GIs were all smiles and waved back, giving a coyote howl. Breeze was starting to like this job.

The girls kept looking better by the minute. They were working on the boardwalk as the trucks slowly moved along with the traffic. He kept his mind on the road and foot traffic, telling himself, *I must be moving in the right direction.* Breeze watched both sides in his mirrors and saw behind him still more men hitchhiking. Others were jumping off. GIs ran into one of the brothels. Three men jumped onto the back of the truck and shouted out where they wanted to be dropped off. Some would just pound on the roof if they wanted to get off. One GI, who got in on the passenger seat, looked at Breeze, who was in shiny new fatigues.

In a very friendly voice he asked, "Are you a brand-new newbie?"

Breeze nodded.

"Well, welcome to Nam! They call me Sketch, short for Sketchdocski. I'm the night guard and perimeter Sergeant, so you'll be seeing me."

If you've been on convoy or were just signing in for your first day, you didn't get guard duty that night; they gave you time to walk around and get the feel of the camp.

Sketch then explained about the area and the people. "But you have to be careful. I'll bring you back here and show you all the right people and places at the right price."

They both smiled broadly, the driver's smile lasting quite a while.

"You're gonna like Saturday nights. Guys come in from other bases and outposts for Saturday Night at the Fights. It's really just a big cookout and wrestling match." Saturday night became a must-do for the troops in the Central Highlands and included a big barbecue. You entertained yourself as best as you could with no electricity, which meant drinking and fights.

Then the small talk changed to where they were patrolling and the size of the area.

Breeze asked, "Is it true we're going into Cambodia?"

"Yeah, we've done that before."

Then he asked about his duties in the company, and he wanted to know the dos and don'ts, and what were the requirements for duty? He wanted to report to the CO and first Sergeant to drop off his 201 file and his orders.

Sergeant Sketch said, "I'll take you to the first Sergeant's office to deliver your orders."

"I have an article 15 court-martial in my 201 file," Breeze said, looking down at the duffle at his feet. "The Army wrote me up for overstaying my leave time. I was a month late in reporting to Fort Lewis for overseas duty. I was homesick, on my first leave since entering the military.

Buck Sergeant Sketch looked at the newbie. "Let's see your orders and the article 15."

Breeze handed him his carrying case, and Sketch pulled out his files. Several minutes later Sketch found what he was looking for and started reading.

Sketch started laughing and looked over at Breeze. "So you stayed home to be the best man for your younger brother?"

Breeze nodded again.

"This was dated ten days ago at Fort Lewis, Washington." Then he pulled the article out of Breeze's 201 file and said, "You know what, we don't do article 15 here." Then he tore the paperwork up and threw the little pieces out the window. This was how you kept your record clean.

"Sergeant Scheffler, our company clerk, will be the first one to see your orders. He would charge you at least twenty-five bucks to do what I did. The First Sergeant would ask you which eye you keep open when you fire your weapon, then he would pop you one, aiming for the other eye. The only copy of your article 15 was the one I just threw out. I won't tell anyone if you won't."

"Thanks, man."

As the truck turned left into an intersection, Breeze had to hold onto the gear shifter. It wanted to pop out of gear with the heavy load and worn-out parts. This was what you did when you drove junk; very different from stateside duty.

CHAPTER 14

*I*t was late afternoon, the end of the day, as they came up to the fuel tanker farm. The guards were changing. Forty men were coming and going around the perimeter. This was the main fuel dump for all of the Central Highlands, guarding thousands of gallons of precious fuel. The fuel tanks were guarded on the ground and in towers night and day. On the right was Artillery Hill. Some of the flatbeds were too overloaded with shells and supplies to go up the steep hill, following the road around and climbing to the back side, which is the main entrance of Artillery Hill. The front of the hill was covered in artillery pieces in camouflage. A mile and a half in front of them was the end of the road and the beginning of the Ia Drang Valley.

As the gun trucks and refrigerated vehicles came up to the front gate, they had to stop and wait for four self-propelled howitzers coming out of Artillery Hill to make their turn and come into the 573. They were preparing to go out in the morning. They were heading for the assembly area for the evening's activities. In the morning the howitzers would go out one of the side gates for duty on a firebase five to ten miles out, always on a hilltop.

The Koreans came for the fights too. The Korean Rock Army had already arrived and were invited to enjoy the evening of food and drink. They had many friends on the base who would share their beer and scotch. Sergeant O'Riley, Tony Lee, and Sergeant

Scheffler were sitting around. O'Riley was going over the shopping list for his men. O'Riley was willing to swap or trade hard-to-find items. Sergeant Scheffler made the arrangements, talking for the 573 supplies that he would swap for the work the Koreans did for us. At night the 573 became a black-market trading post. He was giving a list from Lieutenant Anderson. Scheffler looked it over. It was a lot of items. They talked it over and agreed about the trades in the morning.

Billy walked over. He was happy and talked with Tony Lee, then prepared the fire pit for a large meal. Everyone was in good spirits.

First Sergeant Epler helped with the fire, then he talked to Sergeant O'Riley and Lieutenant Anderson about the supplies they needed. First Sergeant agreed to what O'Riley needed and took his supplies list (food, medicine, chlorine pills to disinfect the drinking water...). Scheffler was standing next to the fire and handed over his list too. Talking over who got what generator and fuel tank, Sergeant Scheffler was going over the details of the sale. He was able to get everything on his shopping list. Like Robin Hood, he would recycle government items, adding 10 or 20 percent for cost-of-living for himself. Sergeant O' Riley would trade one thing for another. He had a long history of being well supplied.

Epler asked O'Riley, "Where are you going with this amount of food and supplies? This is a truckload."

O'Riley replied, "I'll tell you when I get back."

Billy walked around and talked with some of the new personnel. Tripod was with him, looking for something to eat. They both walked into the Blue Dragons' campsite and sat down with all the young cadets who were training for a military career. They were still in their early teens but had decided to become military officers; this was their first step. They too were talking about doing some kickboxing and eating a large steak. As the sun set, more people started showing up, everyone enjoying the company.

It was the one night to make the best out of where you were and what you were. Some sergeants and officers were in the camp for the first time, so there were twice as many as usual. Many new faces, including nine new men from Special Forces, who talked about their new outpost positions on the border. It was a fun night just watching the fire as the stars made their appearance in the night sky. Young soldiers called each other out for a friendly beating.

The Koreans had their campfire right next to O'Riley's. The Americans put out a challenge to the Koreans. It was all in good fun, but this one was for money and the betting began. More wrestling than anything else. The Koreans were in top shape. The young men of the Rock Army didn't speak when fighting; they snorted like a bull, breathed deep, and then snorted louder and louder to antagonize their opponent. They had training and were quick with their hands and feet.

As the evening went on, some of the men from the Special Forces wanted to spar with the Koreans. They were more than ready when Special Forces sent Lieutenant Anderson to challenge for a place in the wrestling circle. The Koreans would do the same. A young Korean captain wanted to make a good impression on everyone. He stood thirty feet behind his troops, then ran up to his fellow soldiers at full speed. They were waiting with hands cupped together. In a gymnastic lift he was launched over the top of his fellow soldiers, landing ten feet away and in the perfect position next to the fire. Then he did another flip all on his own and eyed up his opponent. He waved and signaled with his left hand to Anderson, motioning to him to move closer, to come and get it. They were just sparring and no conflict. The young Korean was very fast and showed his skill with total control, a martial artist student since he was ten years old. Lieutenant Anderson was holding his own. When one got thrown down, he got up and threw the other down. The two soldiers were young and didn't feel the pain. Tumbling around in the sand, trying to get the upper hand, both were very capable hand-to-hand fighters.

It was a clean fight and only lasted the allowable five minutes by the referee, with Anderson and the Korean shaking hands. They enjoyed the evening; everyone was friendly.

Hours went by fast. Everyone ate their fill and enjoyed a drink, steaks, and beer compliments of the Air Force at Cam Ranh Bay and a few chickens thrown in. Some soldiers brought out a sleeping bag and hammock that they spread between the trucks or in the cargo bays. They would all be around a campfire all night.

Two Special Forces sergeants put on their boxing gloves and started calling each other names. This was a grudge fight that could get ugly so Sergeant Epler went over the rules, and everyone agreed to them.

Off to the side, the new Special Forces personnel were getting to know each other. They had their own campsite with steaks and chickens roasting over a spit. Some of the men were sitting on old 175 howitzer barrels, which were laying around in a half circle. This made for a second row of seating. The fire pit was right next to the re-barreling area, where the howitzers were taken to reinstall new barrels. After 100 or 500 rounds (40 feet long), they were no longer accurate so had to be replaced. Four self-propelled 175 howitzers were lined up with their barrels pointed out, with three more 155s (a self-propelled cannon – like a tank but open on the top) also in the circle. The howitzer crews were walking around, enjoying the night and getting to know other troops. They talked about their lives when they were stateside.

Two old sergeants and Lieutenant Anderson were preparing for a ceremony, bringing the new members into their honor guard. The nine new Special Forces troopers were invited to watch the ceremony. You had to be an infantry combat veteran and live through a firefight to become a member of the Honor Guard. Each soldier had to have killed one of his enemies, his first blood – the first man the soldier had killed. You had to cut off several handfuls of his hair and some fingernails, then you dipped it into the dead enemy's blood and wrapped it up to bring it back for the ceremony. The Special Forces and Montagnard scouts had just returned from two weeks of "search and destroy" in Bullet Hole Woods with lots of captured weapons and other equipment. Many larger pieces were airlifted over to Two Core headquarters.

New members watched as two lieutenants and a field-hardened older sergeant stood around the fire pit, preparing tattoo ink in old cans. These three soldiers stood up and talked about the conditions of their battle and taking down their victim. This was how they would be brought into the Honor Guard of Special Forces.

They slowly burned the blood-soaked hair and fingernails, turning them into ashes. Then the ashes were moistened down and made into a paste with Johnny Walker Red scotch, which they used for tattoo ink. This required a separate cooking pot for each individual soldier, usually an old C-ration can. This ceremony brought these soldiers to a higher level inside the Special Forces, a level that was nonexistent in the eyes of white-collar government officials. The tattoo was always put under the right arm so you had to raise your arm to see it. All the tattoos were the same: their blood type in small print of blue or gray or sometimes black ink. This was how they became a full member of the Special Forces upper level, a field commission that was all combat-ready.

They all raised their cups to toast, then took a drink of their "blood," which was always Johnny Walker Red. This was an elite group of combat-hardened assassins. There were only a couple hundred worldwide with no paperwork about them. They were known in higher government levels; some Washington DC personnel and field commanders outside the military knew of them. But there was nothing in writing. They put down opposition and started battles, no questions asked. They were the ghosts of the military. Their motto was "Free the oppressed."

The low-quality, dirty-colored, jailhouse tattoo was only a half-inch square. They were told, never show it to anyone. All of the Special Forces officers and enlisted men had different backgrounds in many areas of the military (radiomen, pilots, scuba men, medics, or just infantry), and they never talked publicly about their duties. Around the campfire the three men, one by one, had been tattooed by three other soldiers who already had earned their tattoo.

As they sat around the fire together, they were invited to plan out the next operation. Everyone came up and gave their congratulations and a handshake. Ten Australian Marines, who called themselves diggers and had been assigned to Two Core, came over and shared their congratulations. Even our new personnel were taking in the ceremony.

Billy came over to watch and also wanted a chance to wrestle. First Sergeant Epler agreed and talked to Tony Lee, who was selling items from our run to the coast to the Blue Dragon Korean Army. Young Billy wanted to find a young Korean soldier who also wanted to have some fun. They put Billy and the young soldier into the sandy pit arena, gave both young men boxing gloves, and explained the rules. There was no betting but there was much hooting and hollering for both sides. Billy was pint-size but he knew how to punch and fight back, a perfect flyweight boxer.

The soldiers liked to prove they were tough but the referee declared no winner. After the match, Billy sat next to his good friend, First Sergeant Epler. Everyone was eating chicken and ham; it was a gourmet meal fried on an open fire.

Captain Shorts was talking to the duty sergeant – the guy on duty who couldn't partake in the party. "We may still need more guns on the outside wall yet tonight, more personnel on all the north and west perimeter."

Captain Shorts nodded in agreement. "We should put more men in the bunkers and half of the company in the second line of sandbags and wait for orders. Every other man should get some sleep."

Sergeant Epler looked around and pointed to two young sergeants. "Bring me the field radio, then tell anyone to start packing weapons and be on alert. It looks like it's going to be a long night."

The reports coming in were all bad, with many requests for artillery. Epler got his field radio and called for a headcount. Keeping track of over 250 of the worst soldiers in the Army was hard enough in the daytime but trying to find them in the dark was even harder. That being done, Epler walked back over and sat down with Billy. Billy heard the conversation and told Captain Shorts that there were more radio calls from the NVA coming in clear today from closer to their base. Epler heard reports from the north and west perimeter of the camp and told Billy to get someplace safe after he was done eating.

The first sergeant had become attached to Billy and wanted to get him back to the states, but he was being stonewalled; all he could do was hope. Epler knew he was going to have to buy Billy's way out.

Fires were burning inside the ring of men, next to the wrestling pit. The Koreans called out their fellow soldiers to fight. It was a good way to work out their disagreements and take out some of their anger. This was better than shooting each other out in the field, which had been known to happen more than once.

Later, Smoking Joe walked into the circle and called out the first sergeant for some boxing. Epler agreed and walked into the circle. He was an equal match. They were both over six foot. Smoking Joe got his nickname from Smoking Joe Frazier. If you saw a picture of Joe Rickard and Smoking Joe Frazier, you would understand. They were practically twins. The first sergeant had always been pretty close to Smoking Joe; Epler and Smoking Joe had talked many times. Rickard's father was also an Army first sergeant.

As they came together, they tapped their boxing gloves. Then they danced around in the sand, doing a couple of head bobs. They started talking and complaining but no name-calling. They were moving around and sizing each other up. Rickard sent in the first left, then an uppercut. He was a second-generation military man. Joe Rickard was two years younger, but Sergeant Epler was twenty years smarter.

Epler said, "I'm going to shape you up with a knuckle sandwich!"

Smoking Joe replied, "You won't be the first or the last!"

Then they both stepped to arms-length from each other and went toe to toe, bombing each other. The first sergeant knew about Smoking Joe's broken ribs but he was a headhunter, going for everything above the shoulders. He was punching in a very uncivilized way – going for broke – no longer dancing in the sand. Both men were hard bodies; they were athletes. It took a lot for the referee to get their attention; there was no let-up. Sweat was flying everywhere, then the referee stepped in and broke them apart after only two minutes. That was the rule. They both needed to be kicked around a little bit, to curb their attitude. They sat down next to each other and removed their boxing gloves. They took a large drink of water, swished it around in their mouth, then bent forward and spat it out, along with some blood. Rickard wanted to go another round. The first sergeant agreed.

As they got back into it, they started bragging about their punching skills.

Epler told Smoking Joe, "If you hit me like that again, I'll send you back to basic training."

He replied, "If I really hit you, I'd send you to heaven."

They smiled at each other and called it quits.

While this was going on Billy went over and talked to Sergeant O'Riley, who was sitting with his friends from the Special Forces. Billy was also a very good friend of Sergeant O'Riley's and had become one of his translators and his civilian material handler, selling military equipment, cigarettes, booze, and gas to the South Vietnamese. He was on O'Riley's payroll and got a small cut of what he sold. O'Riley told Billy, "I'm going to be gone for a month but when I come back, I'll help you and Epler, through my friends in Saigon. I promise."

Billy was also talking to Scheffler about the adoption. They lived under the same roof and had eaten many meals together. They talked about putting in adoption papers again and getting him out and on a plane or a ship, get him away from all this. Get him out before this country killed him. But the Vietnamese government wouldn't give him the paperwork to leave. This had been going on for more than two years. It was the reason the first sergeant re-enlisted, to stay in the Central Highlands.

Sergeant Scheffler knew how to get things done but he couldn't get through the South Vietnamese government. They wanted Billy for their army. Scheffler handled all the paperwork for the entire company out of an accordion file the size of a briefcase. He knew all the under-the-table ways of the Army. One man in the company had grown apart from his wife and did not want to go home and live with her. For a month's pay Scheffler mailed off his death announcement and certificate with a handwritten letter explaining how he came up missing in action. Scheffler wrote a very convincing letter to her and for just another hundred dollars promoted him up two pay grades, all done with a surplus World War II typewriter and military forms the same age.

Billy was different. He had been on the 573 compound so long he spoke better English than Vietnamese. But he didn't know about the pull-out plans. The Army barracks was the only home he knew. US Battalion Headquarters staff (who were split between the different bases) and Two Core High Command were talking about turning him over to the Catholic church in downtown Pleiku. They had other youths living inside their walls already, and the number of survivors and casualties over the years was getting bigger. The church would be safe, and he'd be with his own people; he had to learn the ways of his own people. The Catholic Church in Vietnam was quite respectable and offered him a future.

As the beer dried up and all the fires burned down, the men called it a night. Like it or not, the field radios on the north and west perimeter were calling in activity. There was some shooting several hundred yards past the wire. The men on the perimeter sent up flares and contacted Artillery Hill for a wake-up call, being told to stay close to their artillery pieces. Many reports were coming in that firing was coming in on three locations. The perimeter was being probed for a weak spot.

It was only about eleven o'clock and the CO put more men in the second row of staggered bunkers for the evening. This was nothing new; men didn't mind, unless it was the rainy season. The bunker floor was four feet down and the temperature was cooler there, which made for good sleeping conditions. The old Army mattresses weren't much better than the ground and for a blanket you used your rain poncho and your bulletproof flak jacket as a nice, soft pillow. But there would be no sleeping tonight.

CHAPTER 15

About 2:30 a.m., maybe 3:00, incoming fire picked up on the north perimeter.

Charlie was on the move and wanted in. Yellow and green tracers were hitting the guard towers and sweeping the dugouts that were along the perimeter. They had their spotters in close. The first line of bunkers located their targets, then the firefight started. Orange and red rounds went out, targeting the tree line. Sketch, the perimeter sergeant, wanted to contact the night patrol, which was coming up to the perimeter but was still over a mile out. Sketch got on the radio to the center tower. He wanted to send up a white flare to help direct the night patrol to help get back to camp, and he asked to hold all artillery.

A request for reinforcements came in from the night patrol. All the troops in the camp behind the second row of sandbags and in the dugouts were mobilizing, being called up. In their field gear, squad leaders and sergeants were doing head counts. It was time to move out for the perimeter but they still waited for orders.

Sketch opened up a hole on the perimeter's north wall, then radioed, "Everything away from the north center gate!" Then the outer ring of concertina wire and Claymore mines were carefully moved aside.

Sketch put out the call, "Bring them up in single file and send them out!"

The men moved over the berm, past the wire fence, and hustled their way down into the underbrush on the other side.

More flares were sent up for marking positions.

A call went out, "Reinforcements are in the field with no artillery."

Radio talk was coming in with bad news. The night patrol was being held down. They requested reinforcements again. They were told to keep their heads down but keep moving toward the flares, toward camp. "Three dozen men loaded down with firepower are coming out at a full run and will join up hopefully within forty-five minutes."

Sketch ordered Artillery Hill to put up one flare as a marker for the men in the woods. Artillery Hill used their large guns to send out the flares so they went out father than what we could do at camp with our flare guns. Then he told both the reinforcements and the night patrol, "Move toward the flare so you can meet up."

The reinforcements were coming up to the flare, almost underneath it, and they requested the location of the night patrol.

Coming out through underbrush, climbing a hill, the night patrol was now in contact with the relief team. Artillery spotters with the reinforcements were on the field radios calling in

~ MANG YANG PASS ~

their position, wanting Artillery Hill to drop some rounds behind them. The spotters called in the clicks to Artillery Hill.

The gunnery sergeant said, "No artillery just yet. How many wounded?"

They called in a headcount of all personnel. The rearguard moved to the back of the patrol group to pick up any stragglers.

Sketch told one of the perimeter towers, "And we need two flares in the air every twenty minutes for a return run."

All the wounded were put into rain ponchos for six-man lifts. At this point they all moved out together in a full sprint. We called these men carriers.

Only the rearguard was putting up a fight. The next hour was a nonstop marathon. Soldiers were running side-by-side, each squad always replacing tired runners without stopping. This was done with your red filter flashlight without a word; you rested while you ran. A rested soldier came up behind you and pounded on your back and then moved into that position. There was no stopping for a break. If you fell down or fell behind, another soldier would grab hold of you and bring you along. These six-man lifts were wheelchairs with legs, moving through the brush, over stumps, up and down gullies, through small streams, sometimes pushing and pulling other men. The wounded men who were able to, helped one another, moving through the overgrowth; no man was left behind. The last man was grabbed by his collar, or shoulders. Like army ants you just kept putting one foot in front of the other.

At a full run, they were coming in fast with more firing coming from behind. It was more than just a small probe of VC; it was a full regiment with mortars. They were moving out of the Ia Drang Valley base camp on the Ho Chi Minh Trail. The troops were believed to be the North Vietnamese field unit under the command of General Nguyen Chi Thanh. The Central Highlands offensive line – the Viet Cong – would also be coming out of their mountain caves in the Ia Drang Valley. The Viet Cong controlled most of the area back over the border.

The corner tower shot off flares. There were still more calls coming in on the field radios from soldiers still outside the perimeter. A line of soldiers were slowly coming through the perimeter wire. Personnel were waiting and prepared, ready to help. Dr. Murray and other medics were watching and had a dugout ready to be turned into a temporary first aid station. As they came in, Doc's crew looked them over. The walking wounded were all pointed toward the dugout. The reinforcements were now coming in straight out of the underbrush, from over a hundred yards away. Three and four, then another group. One soldier carried a dead man on his shoulders. He dropped to his knees and looked around. He puts his free hand on the ground, catching his breath. More carriers made their way into camp, grunting and snorting. Other than that, not a word could be heard.

One after another, men followed the flares shot off by Artillery Hill, coming up and out of the darkness to the perimeter. Three more six-man lifts were bringing in more wounded that had come through what was left of the camp's perimeter wire; not even the dead were left. All with no lights and without a word. They regrouped inside the perimeter and set up their weapons to wait to see where the attack was coming from.

The platoon sergeant wanted to make a report to Captain Shorts. Dr. Murray looked him over. "Sit down. You need medical help. From the looks of your arms and legs, you deserve at least three Purple Hearts."

"Charlie's out there and he's hungry tonight. The Viet Cong want us for breakfast."

A very strong force was moving in. Right on their heels the VC were dropping mortars on the entire north and west perimeter wire and marching it in, ten yards forward every volley. Their spotters must have been close, adjusting their firing range and blowing up the Claymores, then adjusting to drop down to the second row of bunkers. They reset again, this time hitting on top of and inside the six-foot berm wire. Small arms fire was already streaking past the US soldiers. Firefighting increased and their foot soldiers broke through the perimeter wire. They were coming strong and fast, and they were directing their mortars farther back into the compound, a sure sign they intended to keep coming. The upper towers had abandoned their posts.

The North Vietnamese had completed the full destruction of our outer defense, blowing up the wire and Claymores. There was no stopping the VC; hundreds kept coming. Bringing up Russian 51-caliber machine guns on wheels, they came across our outer perimeter. They were too strong. We had to pull back from the perimeter and our bunkers. We set up the last line of defense right in front of our hooches.

Captain Shorts called for a fire mission. He wanted Artillery Hill to bring down hell and fire along the north and west side of the whole perimeter, targeting the ground we had stood on twenty minutes ago. The codename for the incoming was Shotguns. Sketch directed Artillery Hill to send out beehives.

The artillery unit had been waiting for the call. The gunnery sergeant shouted out, "Send it!"

Holding onto the ground, the firing crew from Artillery Hill opened up five 105 howitzers and sent out nonstop shelling that was whistling overhead, passing only three or four feet above our positions.

It smelled like burnt waste oil and the shells made the sound almost like hundreds of hissing cats. You could actually feel the heat as waves of arrows passed overhead. No one stood up. After that, artillery sent down antipersonnel rounds, coming in screaming. The ground didn't stop shaking. It was raining mud and pieces of concertina wire ten feet long. The crew on the 175 howitzer shouted orders and prepared to fire. They turned their barrels to the north wall.

The only way you could aim a large artillery piece of this size for close range was to open the breach and look down the barrel, actually eyeballing your target. The four-man crew was sending out rounds at a rate of two per minute. Some of the crew had picked up M-16s and were also firing at anything that moved.

New orders came in over the field radio. It was Sketch.

"Light up the northwest perimeter and send it out at ground level!"

The crew immediately went into action. Shells tore the perimeter berm down to ground level, making short work out of what was left of the concertina wire. One shell landed under a guard tower, knocking it to the ground.

This assault immediately stopped the attack and forced the VC back. They were finally giving up and retreating. More rounds kept dropping in from the VC. Dozens of North Vietnamese had been shot, some only wounded. They helped their wounded move back but were unable to take their dead with them. We started moving forward.

Charlie intended to take the compound before daylight and would more than likely be making another assault. Mortars were still coming in from the NVA. Artillery Hill was directly behind the 573 base, which gave them a perfect line of fire. Sketch was in contact with the gunnery sergeant at Artillery Hill, calling for three rounds of five with 105s. He wanted more beehives down. Then he adjusted their fire. He wanted to march it out ten clicks at a time and send out anything else they had.

From another position farther down the hill, a 30-millimeter pom-pom gun – a double-barreled gun that shot from one side, then the other – opened up on the north perimeter. More beehives from 105s were being sent out. Four rounds of large-size beehives, which were designed to carry farther out, passed overhead. They

~ MANG YANG PASS ~

actually took the air out of your lungs. They hit the ground and shredded. It opened up the underbrush, then smaller beehives were called in for targeting humans, the NVA.

The hissing overhead kept the men in the bunkers or laying down behind the sandbags. An order came down the line to stay down and wait for the howitzers to move to the perimeter. Four self-propelled howitzers could be heard in the total darkness; they approached fifty feet apart. All the foot soldiers picked up and moved behind the vehicles. The howitzer drivers turned their howitzer barrels down so they could fire point-blank over the perimeter. Aiming the 175 howitzers, the first gunner opened up the breach to eye up his target. When you fired at night, you had someone fire a flare. When you saw it land, you pointed the 175 in that direction.

Artillery shells continued to pass overhead. As the gunpower burned away, you could see yellow lines in the night sky. It sounded like jets overhead. Everything on the perimeter had been destroyed; most of it was totally gone from the northwest to the center perimeter. Perimeter guards called to Artillery Hill to send down more beehives with flares along the entire perimeter.

Spotters sent in their request to Artillery Hill for more fire (mortars that would fall closer or howitzers that would fall farther out). More rounds hit. The airport sent out three Cobra choppers, wanting to catch the North Vietnamese retreating. Within five minutes one of the birds was down, shot up with more than ten rockets, only five hundred yards out. Sketch requested another 105 fire mission from Artillery Hill. Captain Shorts immediately sent out a recovery team to the choppers. They used handheld flare lights to light their way. Both pilot and copilot ran toward the camp.

The VC were like ghosts, disappearing into the valley and into the mountains. As always, it was impossible to know which way they went. The Viet Cong knew the planes were coming with bombs. They always fell back in different directions, never retreating in the direction they just came in from. NVA used a J retreat or C retreat. Turning one way or another then turning again. Sometimes the VC were actually behind us but didn't fire on us.

Sketch was on the radio, picking up another US patrol group farther out than the first patrol. He couldn't hear them very well or make out their conversations, but their talking was low and quiet. They were not moving. They were calling for reinforcements and wanted some medics. Doc Murray was standing next to Sketch and Epler. Epler was listening to the call and wanted to know the name of the patrol sergeant. Another call came in. "We need a helicopter."

Epler replied, "They've been shot down as fast as we put them into the air. Couldn't do it till morning! Keep your butts and heads down and stay put. We're coming with reinforcements. How many wounded do you have?"

Epler ran off, leaving Doc to attend the wounded. He only had a minute or two for every wounded man. Doc was applying tourniquets and telling his aides about how we did things in the field. You needed to loosen the tourniquets every so many minutes to keep the blood flowing but then always re-tighten them again to stop the man from bleeding out. The first of two med flight helicopters were dropping in with no lights on, even though Epler tried to call them off. Medics, with the help of ground soldiers, brought in ten badly wounded men. They all needed help getting up to the choppers. Quickly loaded up, the first chopper got back in the air. The second medical helicopter dropped in, and the bird was loaded up.

A call went out to the airport field hospital, on the west of Pleiku, that the American wounded were already underway. A second group of med flight helicopters was coming out but were turned back because another assault was coming in. It would have been suicide; the VC were coming back over what was left of the perimeter.

Captain Shorts, with Sergeant O'Riley and two Special Forces friends, looked over the dead. The NVA all had matching uniforms. All were very young men, just recruited from the north and were regular foot soldiers. Well-supplied fresh troops, the uniform insignias were the 308 and 316th Divisions, all with new AK-47s. Three of them had the same tattoo. It read "Born in the North to die in the South." Stripping the soldiers to check for weapons, a very strange medical observation was made of the young men. They all had been injected with powerful steroids. They had all been dead for an hour or more but still had erections. We knew they had also been given a painkiller and another shot of something very strong, just before they were told to fix their bayonets and attack. It was a suicidal mission, and they felt no pain. The steroids kept their hearts pumping until it was out of the blood. It allowed these young soldiers to take gunshots more than once and kept them moving forward to die.

Epler was organizing five squads to go back out. He was talking with the 573 night-owl patrol and artillery spotter that were caught farther out. They wondered if they could get backup that far out. They were dug in four or five miles out. They were calling for anyone who could help. "Right now we're not taking in any fire but we believe we're surrounded. We need artillery support but we don't know our exact position."

Epler and the CO got back on the field radio and the call went out, "Broken Arrow, Broken Arrow."

This meant retreat, but we didn't call it that. First sergeant Epler wanted a headcount of the night-owl patrol, then he asked Shorts for reinforcements to go out.

The CO gave the order to one of the units that had just come back in, "Back on your feet. Going back out. This time even farther. Double-time it out."

Epler ran back to the bunkers, looking for more of his people, giving the order to volunteer and get ready to de de mow. The men volunteering were the same soldiers that had just come in.

Epler looked at a map, using a compass. He believed there were four hills between the camp and the night-owl patrol. Artillery Hill sent up a long-distance flare using an artillery piece, then shot off another flare while talking with the patrol, hoping to pinpoint their location. The night patrol reported seeing the flare in the distance. This gave Epler and the recovery team a good idea of their whereabouts. They were three miles out, not five.

A twenty-man recovery crew lead by McNulty was on their feet and moving out with only a compass for directions. They were now moving toward what was left of the outside wire; it looked like the face of the moon. With flashlights they moved along in one line, McNulty leading his men straight northwest. The group included two radio men who carried some light equipment. Others carried medical supplies and lots of ammunition. Some put rain ponchos over themselves to protect themselves from the underbrush, which could be sharp-edged. They agreed on communications every thirty minutes, with Artillery Hill sending up flares to mark their location. It was the old way of doing things, but it still worked.

Two hours later, off in the distance, they heard someone blowing a bugle. It was the VC's way to direct their troops. Sound didn't carry very far in this underbrush so the US and VC units had to be close, within a half hour. McNulty believed the US units were maybe only five hundred feet from each other, but in the brush and darkness you couldn't see five feet in front of you. The scouts called to each other in a low voice. Everyone was told, no flares; it would give away everyone's position. Both the night-owl patrol and McNulty's recovery crew sent out scouts for almost an hour. Each group moved through the underbrush, listening, signaling to each other with flashlights with red filters, three long flashes, three short, then three long: S-O-S.

Finally, the comrades met up; the two units came together. McNulty looked over the soldiers and did a headcount. Then he was on the field radio requesting more people and medics. The first duty was to get the wounded up and moving back to camp. As always, the brush was heavy and made it slow going; they could barely walk. They requested more flares to direct their exit. But they were in a valley and didn't see them.

Five complete six-man lifts were formed up and on the way to camp. They positioned one 60 caliber in front, one in the middle, and one for a rearguard, moving the best they could and staying together. An hour later they met up with Tiny, Doc Murray, Cowboy, and me. We brought another five reinforcements for the medical team. We regrouped, took a five-minute break, then all turned and ran for home. Some of the walking wounded were helping by carrying out the more severely wounded.

The buck sergeant in charge of the artillery spotters wanted to take a stand, but McNulty's lead gunner for the reinforcements told everyone Broken Arrow meant to fall back and save the fighting for later. The soldiers called it an attacking but it was actually a retreat. In short, run for it or give them assholes and elbows because that was all they were going to see.

Everyone heard more bugles, this time on both sides of them, and they were close. We heard the enemy but didn't see them. It was a long two miles to the camp perimeter. Men in the towers put out flares to mark our way but we couldn't see them over the treetops. The CO sent Flunky and Bogard out with another group of fresh troops. They were on the field radio, telling us they were coming to help. An hour and a half later, we met up, with the help of the radios. Everyone took a break, and a Navy corpsman came along, looking over the wounded.

Doc Murray was on his knees, using a flashlight with a red

filter clipped to his helmet. It gave him free hands as he applied a tourniquet to stop the bleeding on a man's leg. He knew most of these men and called them by name and congratulated them for not getting killed. Then he told them, "By morning you'll be home for some of the worst food you've ever tasted."

Seeing another medic made Doc Murray happy. The medic was a young, eager college graduate who volunteered for the field and was experienced in keeping someone alive. Doc stood in front of him with blood up to his elbows and pointed where to start helping out.

Doc knew by running with these men he was increasing their chances of bleeding to death. He told them about do-it-yourself tourniquets. At the moment we only had four dead but two more weren't looking good; no help could save them. Everyone was told to throw away anything they didn't need. In total darkness the platoon leaders and Doc Murray ran down the line, checking all the wounded before we ran. Doc was now in charge and giving the orders.

McNulty's scouts were all watching for flares to point out the direction to run. Seeing them far off, all the six-man lifts started heading for home. North Vietnamese foot soldiers were on both sides of us and behind us. Pushing through a small path and around some huge bomb craters, the men on the six-man lifts kept moving forward without a word. The tireless movement was unstoppable. This was what we trained for. When we thought of being a soldier, this was what we came for. If one man fell down, another was taking his place or he could fall out and get some rest but keep the squad of men moving along.

We came to a small trail running along a stream. Here it became an all-out run. We heard small arms fire around us. The NVA fired their weapons as a show of strength. McNulty put his head under a rain poncho and called in a report to let the camp know the strength of the NVA coming at them and that the US soldiers were on their way in. The rear guard with all three of the 60 calibers and six or seven men had quit firing, not wanting to give away their position. McNulty called them, but there was no response. He waited, then called again, but still no response. They were told to call in every thirty minutes. We were still more than two miles out and everyone was getting tired and slowing down.

Seeing the perimeter flares through the tree branches, it was a light of hope. The small arms fire was coming closer, and we could hear another bugle. The NVA were moving forward, shouting to each other while running along. The North Vietnamese must have thought we were part of their unit. They knew they were running alongside other troops but didn't know they were Americans. The darkness and underbrush were hiding us.

The 573 sent out another group with Chico and Shotgun Eddie, who were calling McNulty for his position. The scouts reported back to their squad leader that the two groups had met up. McNulty and Flunky did a headcount. Lefty got on the field radio, hoping to hear a voice from the rear guard. Five minutes later, still no voice on the field radio. That told them one thing, they were all missing. McNulty organized his squad and other volunteers to head back to find them: Flunky, Burnie, me, and some others. We had ten men from two squads turned around and were starting back. We were all told to throw away everything that would slow us down, except for our guns and ammunition. All our flak jackets and steel pots hit the mud. We would be traveling fast and light, backtracking. We didn't know how far we had to go and hadn't had any radio contact for quite a while.

For an hour we slowly and quietly moved through the underbrush. Occasionally, the moon came out and gave us a short glimpse of the landscape. Coming around a bomb crater, our flashlights with red filters helped us find a small trail leading back to our base. Sometime later we heard some talking. We called out and got a return call. We got lucky and found them. The rear guard of six men had gotten overrun. To save their lives they played dead. Three were wounded badly with one dead, Jim Kelly. They were gunned down by some North Vietnamese soldiers who caught up to them. The rear guard threw a 60-caliber machine gun and all their ammo into a bomb crater, which had a foot of water at the bottom, before they climbed in themselves.

We began to carry out men.

The three lightly wounded could move but not run. They were all helping each other. McNulty and several others decided to piggyback the men out. One was willing to try to run by himself. Teams of two and three would take turns carrying the other wounded men. Several men were limping along and refused help. We decided to hide Jim's body. We didn't have enough men to bring him out. Pushing him under several branches of a bush, I took out my Montagnard knife and cut the dog tag off his right boot. I knew Jim so I started talking to him.

In Nam we talked to our dead. We knew they could hear us, and it gave us a feeling that we were not leaving them.

"I'll come back for you. I promise. I'll come back before the maggots get you. And I'll make sure your tag gets to the right people."

We were out of time. Without a word the squad picked up and ran for home. Hearing and seeing rifle fire on both sides again, Lefty went down on one knee under a pair of rain ponchos. He got off a call into Captain Shorts, telling him about the second wave of NVA coming their way. McNulty, like everyone else, was slowing down. All had now been running for more than three hours, out and back. The man on McNulty's back, Roger, was also a personal friend. Roger was half awake and talking to Tom McNulty. The private wanted to stop, but McNulty told everyone that we had to keep moving.

~ MANG YANG PASS ~

"There's a big breakfast waiting for you, Roger, and a clean bed."

We went through a stream, some mud holes, then up a fifty-foot embankment. McNulty took a short break before starting to climb again.

"When we get back to Chicago's south side, I know the place called the Billy Goat. We're going to go together. We'll be lady killers."

He bent over and used his T-shirt to redo a bandage on Roger's leg.

The first morning light was giving us a look of the landscape. We all started clawing our way up the embankment. All of us on our knees, pushing our boots into the muddy soil, holding onto rocks and tree roots, only stopping to catch our breath.

McNulty kept talking. "Don't you die, Roger. We're going back to Chicago's south side and we're going to a Cubs' game. We're gonna watch that lousy football team the Chicago Bears, like it or not. We're going to become gunsmiths and build the best and biggest street sweepers. Don't you even think about dying. We're almost home."

Looking up, two sets of hands grabbed them both. Cowboy and Shotgun Eddie had come back to reinforce the Broken Arrow. Chico and Jerry Jeff jumped over them to get at the men behind them. Fifteen more men came over the hill at a full run. Without a word they put together six-man lifts. Everyone was tired, doing more of a fast walk by keeping their hands locked together to keep moving. Artillery Hill wouldn't send out rounds until everyone was accounted for. It seemed like the North Vietnamese were about to overrun our fortress again.

Artillery Hill sent up flares about twenty yards apart. They wanted all returning soldiers to enter the perimeter between these flares. They kept two or four flares in the air at all times. This was our doorway in. All the soldiers made a path between the flares. The closer we got to their perimeter, the more the ground fire picked up. McNulty and Bogard came upon four more men. With a field radio Sketch called in, wanting to know if they were the very last to be coming out. McNulty said yes. Sketch then signaled to Lieutenant Anderson on the field radio, who was in contact with Artillery Hill, and told him to tell Artillery Hill to send a single round and gave him the coordinates.

Anderson got on the horn with Artillery Hill Master Gunnery Sergeant, who was ready, and requested a single round to be dropped in overhead before firing for effect – before carpeting the area with rounds.

The first men saw the beginning of the compound, which gave them a shot of adrenaline and were double-timing it through the wire and into the camp. Once in, everyone sat down and was given a cantina of water.

Inside the perimeter the soldiers had rolled up four 105 howitzers right next to the 175s. All were aimed at ground level, ready to send out beehives. They were waiting for the last men to come in. Now they got the word, "Send it out."

North Vietnamese mortars started coming in; sandbags were flying everywhere; the soldiers behind the sandbags also went flying.

The officers of the 573 heard a report that the North Vietnamese were attacking all units along the line of defense before the valley leading into Cambodia. The VC prison camp was under siege, the prisoners making an escape. Attacking our positions was a diversion.

The sun was coming up and half the men were told to try and get some sleep and the other half to stay with their guns until morning. Battalion in Two Core wanted a head count of squad leaders, and we were told to do the best we could.

Doc Murray and Shotgun Eddie were with a few others and were cleaning up the wounded and wrapping up in a rain poncho the soldiers who didn't make it. Doc Murray said, "We're running out of ponchos."

A new guy asked the identity of two men. He hadn't been with the company long enough to know who anyone was. The ones without dog tags were identified with the help of comrades before wrapping them up in a rain poncho or Army blanket.. Doc Murray, Sergeant Scheffler, Shotgun Eddie, and I moved the dead personnel who had been identified to the helicopter pad area.

∾

In the morning light, Doc Murray took a last look at the dog tags. Most soldiers had one around their neck and the second one laced up in one of their boots in case their head was missing or the tag got lost. For each man, Doc removed the one from his neck and placed the dog tag between his front teeth and with one kick locked the dog tag between his teeth before rigor mortis set in. This was the Army way in the field. The Army wanted to know who was in the body bag without looking very hard. If a soldier's eyes were open, someone would close them. If he had not been identified, they left their eyes open. This was the way the Army wanted its dead to be turned in.

They would be shipped home in a large tin about seven feet long, welded airtight with no dog tag. The soldiers would be identified through company records. If they couldn't, what was left of them would be sent home as an unknown soldier.

Captain Shorts, Jerry Jeff, and Breeze watched over the wounded. Some were on plasma. They wouldn't be helicoptered out for another hour.

The sun was just starting to come over the treetops, and with it, the Asian heat. Some men were getting some sleep at the bottom of a bunker or dugout. It was cooler and made for a better morning sleep, if possible. For breakfast they passed out C and

K rations, some leftover from the Korean War. The dates on the cans were from the mid- to late-40s. The older they were, the faster they passed through you.

It was Sunday morning. We were getting our first look at what was left of our perimeter. You could see the condition of the perimeter concertina wire everywhere, some hanging from the guard towers thirty feet above the ground. It had been a night without sleep for many men. Some managed a couple of hours off their feet with their eyes open. A major and captain from Special Forces told everyone, "Sit down. Keep down; this won't take long. There is an airstrike coming in."

The North Vietnamese were attacking everywhere in the highlands. Two Core had almost been overrun but had pushed back the assault with the help of the 2nd Battalion 47th Regiment, 22nd ARVN Division – South Vietnamese regulars – commanded by one of their bravest, Colonel Le Cau. The ARVNs were holding their own but taking almost 50 percent in casualties. For the entire day everyone was on the perimeter, guns ready, with Artillery Hill being directed by the 573 where to send out mortars. It was not enough; the attack was still coming. The NVA mortar crews only fired three times in one position then moved, which made it impossible to take them out. While North Vietnamese mortars were dropping in constantly, Army spotters located their position. The Air Force had been waiting and were already on the way with a handful of F105 Thunderchiefs dropping down; their intention was to carpet bomb with one pass.

The F105s came in a V formation, low enough so we could see the pilot looking at us. When the bombs hit, we felt the shock wave as we ducked our heads and covered our ears. After the drop, the air was thick with flying dust, blocking out the sun. The airstrike was close, almost too close. You could smell the gunpowder. Everyone had to dust themselves off and spit out what they had inhaled. No one was complaining. Everyone sat back and waited.

CHAPTER 16

On the third day of the assault things lightened up, and we got our first hot meal from the kitchen. The cafeteria had been hit but it was back up and running, with two walls and no roof. The cooks were back to burning beans. We would eat breakfast outside.

Captain Shorts walked around giving out information and orders to platoon leaders and squadron commanders. He wanted a head count of his men. He also wanted to know who was all involved in the NCO club shooting and bar fight in Cam Ranh. He wanted all the snipers on the gun trucks to come forward. They located me, Lefty, and Shotgun Eddie, along with Bogard.

Shorts said boldly, "You just volunteered to go to heaven."

Then to Epler, "Go find the other sharpshooters and report back in one hour. Meet in front of my office." Then he turned back to us.

"Pad it and back it," he told us, meaning you're leaving on a long trip.

We returned with our backpacks, saluting Epler, Scheffler, and Tripod, waiting for whatever was coming our way. Flunky and Cowboy were brought in off the perimeter, and the last one to be found was McNulty. He was up in a corner tower with his hand cannon, blazing away at anything that moved.

Captain Shorts walked over to where the men were waiting, still eating a can of C-rations.

~ JAMES VOELKER ~

"Take a break and smoke 'em if you've got 'em! You very magnificent seven are going on a long patrol. Leave behind all your weapons or turn them over to your friends. I've got to hide you guys from the shore patrol. They want to put you in LBJ."

Epler went on, "There will be no orders in writing and no waiting around. You'll be leaving within minutes for the airfield."

Flunky, Cowboy, and I looked for someone to hand our sniper rifles to, in hopes of reclaiming them when we came back. Shotgun Eddie gave his rifle to a newbie, telling him how to clean it and keep it in good order. Flunky found Breeze, but he had second thoughts. They did a biker's handshake, then Flunky started talking about the weapon, telling him it shot high at five hundred yards. Everyone found a home for their favorite weapons. Their hand cannons belonged to the gun trucks.

With a final goodbye, Flunky handed over his sniper rifle to Breeze. Back in the states these two would be fighting each other. Flunky and Breeze both agreed if they got home in one piece, they would do a road trip to Las Vegas.

Breeze added, "Another spring road trip. We'll do the road to Mardi Gras in New Orleans. Bourbon Street!" Then he started bragging. "I had an amazing chrome-plated chopper with a teardrop tank with the American flag painted on it. I hand-painted it myself. Only one like it on the west coast."

With that the seven men loaded up gear and equipment, with three Special Forces helping out. Two cargo helicopters with a Cobra gunship escorted our liftoff. It was a short ride to the airport in Pleiku, which was right next to the hospital. All the airport landing pads were being used so the two cargo helicopters dropped down over a flat roof. Everyone threw their gear out, then jumped out. We threw our packs to the ground and jumped off the tin roof. Medical personnel from the hospital were coming and going. We saw Doc Murray helping the nurses and doctors. He had been shot in the leg and was limping around, but he didn't have time to complain. He was waiting on the next set of helicopters to drop down other medics to help take care of the backlog of patients.

Watching as the Red Cross birds shut off their motors and the rotary blades come to a stop, we saw nurses run out to the landing pad. They too were wearing steel pots and flak jackets. The wounded were being quickly offloaded. The choppers couldn't wait; they were targets, and besides, they had to go back out again. There was not enough personnel to carry the wounded in. We dropped our backpacks and began carrying the wounded on bamboo stretchers. We realized these men were from much farther out. There were also some Special Forces and South Vietnamese regulars. Brought out on foot and traveling for several days, all the soldiers had open wounds and had fly larva moving under what was left of week-old bandages made up of old pieces of clothing and uniforms. They smelled like death warmed over.

We brought the wounded inside; the floor in the hospital was red with blood. We couldn't do much more. Lieutenant Anderson came in and pointed us toward the airplane assembly area. It was only a short walk. When we reached it, we helped unload a supply truck. We were joined by Sergeant O'Riley and his men, including Lieutenant Anderson and Tony Lee. O'Riley was not wearing his usual uniform; he had on tiger-stripe jungle fatigues and was wearing the rank of colonel. All the Special Forces men were captains or lieutenants. That's when we found out this was O'Riley's game.

"We'll be gone for a month. If you want to get off a letter, do it here," he said.

"You have about two and a half hours before we take a C130 to Takhli, Thailand. Once we get there, we'll tell you more."

All of us sent off a letter. I wrote to my brother.

I'm not going to pay that IOU. If I die, you better hope for me.

~ JAMES VOELKER ~

Then I got another letter off to Sergeant Scheffler.

I've hidden my hand cannon and some gold bars I purchased in a downtown shop.

I told him where they were, then I added a line or two to other friends in the company.

O'Riley had us offload dozens of other equipment containers. We realized this was going to be our job; we were going to be the mules to carry all this. But it was better than listening to the shore patrol in the Navy's jail.

Everything we offloaded was put onto an Air Force C130. O'Riley did an equipment check, then a head count and gave the okay to the pilot and copilot. "Tell everyone to buckle up, then start to taxi to the end of the runway!" Then he called in the flight information for the trip to Takhli.

It was a short hop for the C-130, and we were back on the ground in no time, where we stayed for the night.

∽

In the morning we were told we were moving into smaller planes, and everything had to be offloaded and loaded onto the four smaller Dornier Do-28s that were lined up one behind another on the tarmac. Flunky offloaded the C-130. Cowboy and Lefty were doing the legwork between the planes. Shotgun Eddie and I loaded the cargo into the smaller planes. McNulty and Bogard were stacking the cargo tight, not wanting to waste any space. All four of the Dornier Do-28s were transport planes with no markings, compliments of the CIA and owned by American Airlines out of the Udorn airbase.

When the C130 moved off, O'Riley spoke. "We're going on a one-month walk in the back country into Burma."

~ MANG YANG PASS ~

With that we all got on the plane and headed for Mandalay, Burma (today known as Myanmar) with no questions asked; we just looked at one another. Everyone was asking themselves, what did we get ourselves into and how do we get out if things go wrong?

∞

Some hours later, the planes landed in Mandalay, where we spent the night. In the morning we were told about our next stop, a small base in Bhamo. Then we were to go into some backcountry mountains and the beginning of the Burma Road. We would go in country by truck and backpacking on foot to the Chinese and Burma border.

Lieutenant Anderson told us, "We've done this before; it's a walk in the park, a very long walk in the park."

Then as we walked over to a set of tables inside an airport hangar, we could smell the food. We were told we were going to meet some members of the Burma government, some dignitaries. Several Burmese officers appeared to be well off. Other government people, possibly military, were greeted by some other Burmese officials. O'Riley, Anderson, and Tony Lee were given one interpreter and two scouts. O'Riley, and some of the other crewmen, seemed to know the scouts.

The officials exchanged some paperwork and told us the names of our guides and that they had all the maps. While still talking, a car pulled up and another group of officials walked in, possibly an ambassador from India; he seemed to be dressed in that manner. All government personnel from Burma and India traveled with their families. A handful of well-dressed officials came over and shook hands with the US crew.

One of the officials had his daughter as an interpreter, a

government family member. Her name was Aung San Suu Kyi and she said to us, "Be safe in Burma. Always listen closely to your guides. We have no radio contacts that far out, only the tribes and loggers. If you get into any trouble, you're on your own."

The Mandalay airport was busy, but we were kept out of sight, down in one of the hangars owned by Burma's government. We were given a very big meal, then Aung San, with the other government officials, sent us off with a smile and a goodbye.

All four of the Dornier Do-28 planes took off, heading north to Bhamo, a small town with an airport in the middle of the foothills.

When we landed, we found out they had made arrangements for a large all-wheel-drive truck to take us the rest of the way to Wanling. Mandalay was our last sign of roads with pavement; it was the last of our easy traveling. From then on it would be all mud roads. The next leg of our journey would bring us to the village of Bhamo. The truck was fully supplied from the planes. A half dozen AK-47s and the dozen English, single-shot, bolt-action sniper rifles with long range scopes were offloaded but kept in their wooden containers. O'Riley, along with five other people, helped offload the equipment into the all-wheel-drive truck. He told us that they were now working for the CIA.

Flunky looked over to Bogard and me, smiling and said, "Great, back in California I'm wanted by them and had people looking for me. Over here I'm working for them. They must not have done a background check on me."

O'Riley had been in the CIA for almost five years. This was his third trip back to Burma, with the same crew each time: Tony Lee, two radio men, and Lieutenant Anderson, who was O'Riley's right-hand man. The group was specially organized just for this trip. Many of the men hadn't seen each other since last year. There was talk about their headquarters in Washington DC and their promotions, if everything went well. Anderson talked about the trip in. We would be going uphill all the way.

"We need you men. In some places it's straight up. We're heading for the Chinese border to make a movie. A spy mission. We're going to photograph the Chinese Army in their New Year's Eve parade. This is the year of the monkey."

We were all packed. It was time to move out. Everything was going as planned. We piled into the back of the all-wheel-drive truck. Bhamo was not that far but the old Burma Road had ten or more switchbacks and hairpin turns. Most of the road was in need of repairs. The natives used oxen carts or even elephants for transportation. Only major repairs had been done since the end of the rainy season when the road narrowed down to one lane of traffic. All drivers had to get out and inspect what was left of the road for their own safety. No one traveled the road at night.

The road had been repaired very little since the end of World War II, and it had all been done with hand tools. The villages provided day laborers, who were all Buddhist and believed every, time they moved a shovel of dirt, they had to recite a short prayer, then remove the earthworms, so as not to kill them or harm them. Their religion declared all life sacred. With those road conditions, it took more than a half day to reach the outer streets of Bhamo. The people there were all friendly and curious and wanted to trade whatever we could offer them.

At this point the all-wheel-drive truck had paid for itself, as we went north, offroad on some old logging roads. By nighttime we came to our last stop, a village and our new base camp. The village had no electricity, and everyone was gathered around large fires in the center of the village. We were with the tribe of Palaung, in their main village. This was a rural village. The men raised livestock, and they had dozens of elephants that were trained for the logging. They were the best work animal for these rugged hills.

The west side of the village was up against a steep rock cliff with an opening in the trees, bringing in afternoon sunlight. One side of their homes became part of the fence. The other two sides had an eight-foot fence of solid timber with a large stream of fresh mountain water for the animals' water. The holding pens for the livestock were very roomy with sand and stone floors. The elephants kept the village clean with the help of the young people, who were their trainers and full-time guardians. All the elephants were treated like family; all had names. After they were twenty weeks old, the small elephants were assigned to one of the men in the village.

Some of the villagers had been recruited to guide and travel with us on our trip. The guides knew this area and were bringing tools for mining. Their main interest was rupees and they used the elephants to move material of all types. The Palaung women of the village had a very unusual tradition; their necks and ears were stretched out with copper coils. The hundred-year-old tradition was to make them beautiful, and it distinguished them as being from the Palaung tribe.

We set up camp, then walked down to the large pond for a swim with the young people and elephants. It was a gathering place for everyone from the village. The mountain water was crystal clear, and you could see fish down by your feet. The water was cooling. Everyone came down to get away from the heat. We would rest here for a day and get organized with our guides. No need for the guns here. We kept them wrapped and locked up in the cab of the truck for safety. The village children were into everything. The villagers believed children could do no wrong.

We saw more and more young girls. All wore copper rings around their necks. No young men did this.

O'Riley and his two radio men had set up their field radio equipment. Their interpreters and scouts were all sitting around in a circle, getting the information they needed to start out. They

~ MANG YANG PASS ~

were picking up a local radio station and enjoying the music and the weather forecast. In the morning the Palaung tribe were going to be traveling up country to one of their logging camps. This would be the first leg of our walking journey. The guides would be bringing nine or ten pack animals and just as many elephants for the first two days. The Palaung tribe was sending out supplies to several of their logging camps along with us.

O'Riley intended to mix in with the supply transport and move along with them. He had traded new chainsaws with the loggers for their assistance with our journey, a very welcome trade and a valuable piece of property for the loggers, who exported teak logs. The two interpreters were preparing the last details and mapping before we moved out. O'Riley had given the village another gift, a very small generator, which they had no use for because they had no electrical appliances, but they wanted to keep it. They were moving into the new world and liked it. Knowing this, Colonel O'Riley also presented the village chief with a four-band radio, capable of picking up news and weather. The new equipment brought in all the young people, who were very interested in the outside world. They also wanted a field radio so they could talk back to other villages. They realized their lives were going to change before their eyes, and they wanted to know more about the outside world.

Some were starting to send their children to schools with the help of government officials. He also gave them an assorted variety of hand tools and some much-needed equipment and gasoline.

One interpreter spoke Burmese and American and told the village chief, "Thank you for helping." He had family in the village and many friends. He was young but excited and very much enjoying his adventures, getting to know his new American friends. He was looking forward to their adventure. The others spoke Chinese, Burmese, and some English. Six village men traveled along to help with the livestock.

After the morning conference, the equipment was offloaded from the truck, then the vehicle was covered up with vines and branches so as not to be seen from the air. All equipment was loaded onto water buffalo and elephants. Two hours later the hike began.

Chapter 17

For most of the trip we would be living off the land. We had been given rifles but were told the Burmese guides would do the hunting. They used old 22 rifles, which O'Riley supplied to them with lots of ammo. Moving out of the camp, we realized why they had to leave the truck behind. The Burmese loggers had engineered a watery trench down the center of the road. This helped move the huge teak logs using as many as four elephants. Workers were coming and going in both directions.

After three days of almost all straight uphill, moving into the Nujiang Salween territory, we slowly wound our way up and down along a steep hill. The entire group came around the corner of a large outcropping of solid stone. The guide told us this was the start of the new landscape. Everything changed from a wooded hillside to an overgrown forest of vines. As the day went on, the vines overtook almost all the trees. The vines had become as big as the trees. There was no getting off the trail; the vines were too thick.

We spent the entire day hiking and chopping through the underbrush, usually walking down the center of the small stream. As the day turned into evening, the scouts looked for someplace high and somewhat dry. Everyone's spirits were up as we started a fire and set out our hammocks. O'Riley informed us it was only a day's walk to our final campsite. The cook prepared the usual meal of monkey meat and enough rice cooked up for everyone. With some water to make tea, we also opened some C-ration containers of bread and called it a day.

Hanging up our mosquito nets, we heard grunting and groaning and saw movements along the trail. The old guides told us not to do any shooting. It was only the natives coming out to see what we were doing. At this point a great ape stood in the trail only fifty feet away with two more coming out of the trees and vines, not coming forward, just watching us. The guides told us the apes were just being curious, and they would be with us the entire time. "This is their homeland and sanctuary. Some of them will follow us around, but don't try to make them into a pet."

∽

In the morning, the sunlight opened up the trail, and the men got up and saw a large number of red apes on the trail, watching us and following the water buffalo. Younger ones were brave enough to come into the camp. The scout and interpreter told everyone, "The group seems to be the same group as last year."

Small baby apes came over to shake hands with one of the Burmese. In broken English he told us, "These two are always together. I can tell by the white under their chins. They're probably brother and sister. Some of the other ones were here last year too but were only half that size. They're growing up very well."

More young ones were coming in for a handout. Some older ones slowly walked into camp and started talking to each other and had their hands out, then sat down for a casual look around.

O'Riley told us not to shout at them or try to scare them. They loved to watch and actually made very good guards. This was why no one came here. This was a sanctuary. The Burmese and Chinese considered the apes to be their ancestors. They were called the forest people. The apes lived on the mountaintops above us. They were down here for water and some plants to eat.

"And don't feed them or you'll never get rid of them." O'Riley looked around and shook his head. "See what I mean? This furball here remembers me from last year. I gave him half a candy bar. He's been following me around as if he knows I've got the other half."

The great apes were coming in close; all seemed to want to help. They actually started petting the water buffalo.

Colonel O'Riley wrote in his notes and daily register. He knew McNulty was also keeping a journal and told him not to use officer's names or places and dates, and not to mention the CIA, which McNulty agreed to, telling O'Riley, "That doesn't leave much except for the furballs."

On the sixth day, as usual, the sun was up. Our friends the Asian apes joined us, slowly moving with the pack animals around large stones. By midmorning the landscape began to change. As we walked steadily, the hillsides became cliffs, up on both sides. Even though we were walking uphill, the canyon walls were growing and closing in. Looking up, it appeared to be a hundred feet or more to the top. You could only see a sliver of sunlight. We kept walking for over an hour, walking on bare stones along the stream.

Coming around a sharp right turn, we were stopped by a waterfall and had to offload the pack animals and push all the containers by hand up and over what looked to be a set of man-made stairs. The water buffalo were slowly brought up after. Later, we came to a fork in the path. O'Riley's guide pointed us to the trail along the cliff. The other trail turned and followed a large pond. Farther back you could see another waterfall in the far-off distance. This was where we would leave all the pack animals. It was almost straight up, but this hike saved two days of walking.

O'Riley oversaw the equipment being off-loaded, and they

told everyone, "When we reach the top, we'll be back in full sunlight and will be able to enjoy a great view of China." Then he added, "Be very careful. We can't replace anything out here."

Lefty and I strapped long containers to a pole, which we shouldered. This was where the seven volunteers got to work to earn their pay. We unloaded the last water buffalo and backpacked all our cargo. We all stood around, looking up, watching the mountaintop.

Lieutenant Anderson and Colonel O'Riley turned to us and said, "Let's go."

We began our climb. As usual McNulty wanted to lead the team. There was no footpath. They sent out three scouts to see which one could find the easiest way up. Flunky and Bogard found a path up against the cliff just wide enough for one person. They called to everyone to come over and do the same. Shotgun Eddie and Cowboy carried huge packs using walking sticks. For the next three hours we wound our way up and around rocks and boulders. The guides were scouting ahead. They reported back and talked to the other guides about which way they preferred to go. There were three trails and none of them would be easy. They also said they wanted some meat for supper. They would have to shoot a half-dozen monkeys to feed all of us.

They agreed on one trail. We kept moving while it was still daylight. The first climb took us up to four switchbacks and then to a rocky edge, where we had to use ropes to climb up in several locations. The climb went up more than a hundred feet of almost sheer rock. When we reached the top half, we were sent back for two more trips for what remained. The entire day was spent rock climbing, pulling ourselves and the equipment to the top of the plateau.

O'Riley didn't wait. He went out ahead of us. Leading four men over the hill and through the tree-covered underbrush, where they had a view of the valley below. It was over two miles from what appeared to be a good-sized city. There didn't seem to be any logging going on or much of anything else. O'Riley, with some of the other CIA personnel, had field glasses and began to scout the mountaintop. A short while later we joined them, bringing in the equipment. The officers started to unload and clear a path to several large trees. They brought out some hatchets and started cutting small trees toward the second and third large tree. Using machetes, we cut off lower branches, then O'Riley requested a volunteer to climb the tree and give us a report of the view of the city. Tony Lee volunteered. He climbed and chopped off branches on his way up. Suddenly, he came across a wooden ladder from prior years.

Anderson and five other men brought up the containers to start building a treehouse. O'Riley, Cowboy, and McNulty assembled oversized binoculars and telescopes. When the treehouse was ready, they moved everything up. I set up binoculars and cameras. The other men constructed three more treehouses using many of the logs from last year. In no time we stood and looked out over the valley. Looking down at a city named Wanling, it was a beautiful city and beautiful view.

We were half in China and half in Burma. O'Riley's men then assembled a large tripod and 35 mm camera with a three-foot-long field telescope. One of the CIA officers informed everyone to keep all the camping equipment on the backside of the hill. No fires or smoking in the treehouses, only in low spots where they couldn't be seen. The scouts and guides worked together, chopping their way over to a fairly flat area made up of limestone where it was dry. They set up camp, believing we would be there for about ten days. The interpreters opened up a short-wave radio, tuned it to the local music station, and started listening for the weather report. In the local news most of the Burmese people spoke a little of both Burmese and Chinese, which was almost the same as Chinese.

O'Riley wanted everything in the campsite to be camouflaged or on the backside of the hill. Anderson and Cowboy opened up other metal containers and brought out a small cook stove. Out along the cliff several of the men had climbed another tree, which looked to be the oldest. The majestic old tree had a massive root system and trunk and looked like an octopus holding onto the stony edge of the hillside. You had to walk under three layers of roots then climb up through loose stones and dead branches to get to the trunk. Its base was well rooted but it leaned over toward a dropoff of several hundred feet.

It made a great observation post but was not easy to get to. From there we could view the main road. We stopped looking for another good position; the view of the city was excellent, and you could see across the valley to the next hillside.

The Palaung tribesmen set up camp. The tribesmen were all very interested in the stream further back. Later, after all the hard work was done and campsite set up and completed with the treehouses for viewing, most of the Palaung men walked down the hill for water. They also brought out shovels and flat pans. The tribesmen intended to search for rare metals and pan the stream for rupees, and they spent the rest of the week doing so.

When all the camera gear was set up and camouflaged with rain ponchos and branches, O'Riley and his men had a long look at the city they were going to photograph. McNulty had his journal with him and was catching up on his calendar of events, something he enjoyed doing even though he couldn't mail it off to anyone for a month. Out here officers were treated like enlisted men up to a point. Lieutenant Anderson assigned Bogard, Flunky, and Cowboy to set up three new observation towers. The weather was good; the view into the city couldn't be better.

Later in the day Shotgun Eddie and I went with Lieutenant Anderson to scout along the edge of the cliff, a short patrol just to get to know our surroundings. The crew chopped wood to make

~ MANG YANG PASS ~

another treehouse and camouflage in another tree, which was also rooted over a different stony edge and pointing toward the northwest and the main road leading into the city. While working on detail we noticed, coming out of the forest along the cliffs, our friends the great apes. They had taken the long way around, avoiding the steep cliffs. It took them almost an entire day to catch up.

The apes all walked to our camp together. The scouts wanted to know what trail they came off from. Nosing around the camp, the apes went through the open containers, then started walking around. They liked the three treehouses as much as the camera men did. Men took turns coming up to view the city through the field telescope.

Anderson and one of the captains brought out two even bigger cameras that they wanted assembled in the treehouse overlooking the main part of the city. This camera was over five feet long. Only the CIA people were allowed to operate it.

After we finished assembling the treehouses, O'Riley told us to make up our own hours for guard duty. Two men would sleep in hammocks in the treehouses every night, a relaxed guard duty. McNulty and Flunky agreed to start the first shift.

For the next two days all the CIA people took turns watching the city and listening to the local radio channels. The radio gave us information on the events of the upcoming New Year's parades and the Lantern Festival.

The Chinese New Year is always from the new moon on the first night of the lunar month and ends on the full moon fifteen days later. They only had two or three days until the full moon. Already the sound of music could be heard, and many of the streets were starting to glow with lanterns. The Chinese were celebrating in the streets and had outside fire pits for cooking and enjoyment. From the hilltop we could see dozens of smoking fireplaces mixed with fireworks. The Chinese enjoyed a feast and their family reunions during this yearly tradition. The New Year festival had begun.

The second morning small amounts of fireworks were going off around the city. By afternoon it was everywhere.

That night the radio was alive with music and events. We could see street dancing through the telescope, and fireworks were always in the air.

O'Riley said, "Tomorrow is the day things will start. Lots of music and announcing who's going to speak at the festivities for the next week, possibly ten days."

Throughout this celebration the Chinese government spoke every morning with a call of unity for the people. The local mayor would announce a list of upcoming events in different parts of the city, give small speeches, and the small businesses and street vendors advertised their wares throughout the day.

In the main square the parade started off with a red paper monster, a fire-breathing dragon that the translators said was named Nian. They said that Nian was a mystical beast, a storybook character passed down from great grandmothers and grandfathers. He was fifty feet long and weaved his way from one side of the street to the other. With him came fireworks, which was symbolic and was supposed to scare his dragon spirit away, along with shouting and singing. Then came the dancing lions with more fireworks. The grand finale would be at midnight. Lastly were the flags and the city's orchestra on parade.

O'Riley and Anderson recorded the mayor's speech off the radio. Military personnel were the next to speak. All morning and far into the afternoon all the streets were busy with soldiers and civilians coming and going, waving flags and setting off fireworks. As nighttime came, the fireworks overtook the public square.

For the next nine or ten days many different military men and woman and youth groups from the government spoke. All the CIA people had been waiting for a military parade, which was about to start. Looking through both field glasses, they photographed the city below.

Cowboy and I were in the treehouse with Lieutenant Anderson. Cowboy asked the camera crews what they were looking at. The captain replied, "It's the city of Wanding. We will see a display of their newest and best missiles, with new equipment, tanks, and dozens of heavy artillery. There are missile launchers at the end of the procession, along with ten new vehicles that looked to be Russian. Colonel eyes them up. Each has been outfitted with a satellite dish or possibly radar or a microwave of some type. O'Riley wants each truck photographed. Behind them are more troops, about a half million Chinese soldiers in total, all in uniform marching through the city. This was what we came to see."

For the entire day they filmed the parade using the movie cameras, and they photographed the entire parade that showed off their military equipment and readiness.

The military parades continued for two days, lasting over six hours each. With singing on the radio, flags flew up and down the streets. Fireworks continued all day, and by night the entire city was glowing again. O'Riley told us that tomorrow was the grand finale, signaling the end of the parade and the beginning the year of the monkey.

By noon on the last day, there were fireworks again, and even more military personnel parading through the streets. These appeared to be Chinese Navy personnel, singing songs about victory. The lieutenant, with one of the captains, was filming and photographing every bit of the city.

The young soldiers in uniform – a white shirt and red bandanna around their neck – were singing the national anthem and waving. Everyone took turns viewing the grand finale. As Lefty took his turn, he turned the telescope to the forest. Across the valley he noticed movement on the hillside. People in uniform were looking back at him through their binoculars: Chinese soldiers in full field gear, weapons ready. They were looking and pointing in our direction.

"Lieutenant, you may want to look at this. We've been found."

The lieutenant took a quick look.

"Jesus H. Christ!" He turned back to Lefty. "Go find O'Riley and the other CIA officers, now!"

Chapter 18

When O'Riley reached the treehouse and looked through the scope, the Chinese soldiers were still watching us. Another group of Chinese soldiers pointed to our position. They appeared to be on their field radios and had brought out a map, pointing in the direction they intended to travel.

Both interpreters got on the radios and listened for anything. O'Riley ordered to quickly break up camp and move out, but we had to keep everything out of sight.

"We're going to move out and be gone in fifteen minutes."

The pack animals were quickly loaded up, and we started back down using the longer trail, a much longer route but it moved us directly away from the Chinese soldiers. It was same path our ape friends came in on.

As we moved along a path, we heard a plane in the distance. We ran into the underbrush and hid. The great apes thought it was a game, and they came in and sat next to us.

A small plane dropped down to almost tree-top level, flew overhead, turned around, and flew overhead a second time. The Burmese interpreter was picking up the plane's radio transmission to his base headquarters. They believed we were visitors, travelers for the New Year's Eve celebration.

The plane gave out our location, so the Chinese Army continued to pursue us into the apes' sanctuary. On the field radio we could hear them trying to make contact with other troops, who were farther into Burma, then the radio went silent. With no break or rest, we hiked alongside the steep cliff, then down to a stream.

O'Riley called out, "Double time it. We're going to run like smoke."

This way back was almost totally downhill. The guides and translators watched the sky for the plane to come around for the third time. The plane never returned.

The translators kept monitoring the field radio. Some of the transmissions were the Chinese calling out, wanting to talk to anyone with a radio. They wanted to know a location and description of the travelers. They called out to us too, wanting to talk to us and find out just what we were doing.

O'Riley instructed the interpreters not to talk. They received another call. It was Chinese patrols. They thought that we were also a Chinese patrol and wanted to hook up so they requested our location.

O'Riley now knew we had Chinese soldiers in front of us, which meant we had to change direction.

It was still morning. The guides told O'Riley about another path that was longer but never used. Most of it ran down the middle of a stream. It was the dry season and would be safe until we came to the river. In the wet season you had to use a raft.

O'Riley and the other CIA people agreed, then turned and moved out. Lefty, Bogard, and McNulty were packed up with camera gear on their back and a rifle over their shoulder. Using their free hand, they chopped their way down the path with a machete to what they hoped was a small stream.

The scouts called this the Valley of the Vines. No one used this overgrown elephant trail. It was a narrow, rocky path through the vines, very slow going with no level ground and many places the sun could not penetrate the vines. The apes would not follow us in.

O'Riley and his people decided to send half the tribesmen and water buffalo down the elephant trail with no American equipment, hoping that they would meet up with the Chinese. There would be no questions about who they were and why they were there. The Burmese agreed and would rejoin our group later or every few hours send a messenger back and forth.

The entire day machetes were needed for chopping our way along the steep hill. The day went fast, and as nighttime closed in, the vegetation was so thick the darkness came early. Being tired, wet, and dirty, everyone was more than happy to look for a level piece of land. We set up camp and turned on the local radio and walkie-talkies, hoping to hear some news or possibly even a weather report. We spent the night around a small campfire under the canopy of overgrown vines.

When we woke up in the morning, there was a strong fog, so everything around us was wet. We decided not to wait for the sun. We were already wet down to the bone. It would take all day to burn off the heavy morning fog. We had to keep moving. The guides told us there was only music on the radio and almost no talking. They also told us the stream was only five hours away, and we would spend the rest of the day walking south, downstream, taking only one break for something to eat.

Late morning two scouts came back from downstream. The water was only a short walk and with a big smile they told everyone we could catch a large amount of fish for our next meal. As soon as we reached the stream, we realized it was more like a small river. Since it was flowing too fast, we had to build some fairly strong rafts for all our equipment. Tribes knew which type of wood was the best for rafts, so everybody began construction. As the last raft was completed and loaded, we all pushed off together. As we walked and floated alongside, we realized this was actually the best way to move, and much easier than having twice your body weight on your back.

For the rest of the day we pushed through the heavy vines in the narrower stretches and mud in shallower stretches and went around several turns. Another smaller stream from the northwest connected up with a small waterfall. The stream straightened out, and the landscape began to flatten as the river turned south. Then we heard human sounds and felt the presence of other eyes watching us.

Coming up to a bend in the stream and appearing on an upper sand bank stood three Chinese soldiers, possibly lieutenants with more than two dozen well-camouflaged Chinese soldiers. They came out of the underbrush and walked toward us.

One of them called out in English, "We finally meet up. Been looking for you for two-and-a-half days."

O'Riley and his Special Forces lieutenants were more than surprised. They all glanced at each other, hoping for the best.

One Chinese officer introduced himself. "I am Wes." Then he turned and introduced his officers and men with a handshake and a friendly nod of the head.

Wes, a well-to-do Chinese captain with two of his lieutenants and his sergeants, was the first to shake hands. They all told us their names in English.

All officers had trained in Japan and had traveled to the United States so were very excited to talk to the Americans. One officer told us his mother was half Chinese half American and lived in Chinatown in downtown San Francisco. He loved the West Coast and had had four years of college in history and English and was working on a degree in law. He said the Chinese government may send him and his family back to the United States as a Rhodes Scholar once he finished in one of the Midwest colleges.

The Chinese captain didn't seem to want anything. Telling Colonel O'Riley and his lieutenants, "You don't have to sneak

~ MANG YANG PASS ~

around to come to our New Year's Eve parade. We have been watching you for three years."

O'Riley and Anderson looked at each other in amazement.

The captain continued. "China is beginning to open up its borders. My orders were to see you out of the country unharmed. We will help you carry out your equipment. My father was an officer in the Chinese army. For years he served his country. I am going into government law in hopes of becoming an ambassador to your country. My background and schooling brings me here to you, and hopefully we have a happy meeting. Today my sister and two cousins are attending college in the states; one is going to Stanford and loves football games. When she returns, she will run a section of our government. One is going to Harvard and may not want to come home as she wants a double citizenship. My young cousin is a party animal at the University of Wisconsin and does not want to come home. Every family has one of those.

"China uses Hong Kong University and Taiwan University to send our young students over to the United States. Myself and two of my officers were born in Hong Kong and have Chinese and English citizenship. In the future we hope to do more on both sides."

The Chinese captain smiled and said, "The world is getting smaller every day. The People's Republic of China is looking to the future for its people."

Then he started talking about how fun the Chinese New Year's had been and how they had to miss a lot of it to come up into the sanctuary and search for the Americans.

The Chinese soldiers had a fire started and were opening up cans of their favorite seafood. Two others cut up red onions and placed them in a pan while passing out containers of crackers for a gourmet luncheon for both field units. It smelled like home cooking, complete with rice.

Everybody was hungry, and in no time the soldiers had eaten

everything. Not wanting to break up this get-together, they talked for a while about the world, but realized we had to go in different directions, otherwise this lunch break could have taken us the rest of the day. A large number the Chinese spoke fairly good English and they liked to talk about their experiences in life. They bragged about how far and how great China and Burma were and how they planned to become a modern and educated country in the years to come.

"We had a border with no rules or guns. In one hundred years we will be one people."

After everything was eaten, the Chinese helped the Burmese put everything back on the rafts. Then Wes called to one of his lieutenants to bring up the field radio and he made a call into headquarters, asking for his duty list for the day. He was told to return to base camp and give a full report. He signed off and talked to his lieutenants, who in turn gave the order to the men to start picking up equipment to move out. Then they lined up, gave us a short goodbye, and began to backtrack. We pushed off and started floating again. The team of water buffalo followed behind, moving downstream. After three hours we entered the forest country where we saw more wildlife. The stream widened out. We walked and floated in waist-high water. The water buffalo had no weight on their backs and were very used to the water.

There were less vines on the teak trees so more sunlight filtered through the canopy. It was getting toward dusk, so we talked about setting up camp for the night. Wes, the Chinese Captain, was on the field radio saying goodbye and telling Colonel O'Riley to write down several addresses of his family stateside, asking him to please send them a postcard for him. Lieutenant Anderson chose a sandbar with tall grass, a dry spot for the evening. Everyone helped make camp, then the interpreters set out their radio gear, hoping to hear some music or maybe some voices, but we were too far out.

~ MANG YANG PASS ~

On the walkie-talkie they picked up Burmese conversations between logging crews, so we figured we were getting close to a camp. They gave up listening for the day and made plans for tomorrow.

In the morning we continued down the stream, and by midmorning we saw trees that had been cut down and a well-used elephant trail. We pulled the rafts onto the shore and made plans for the day.

Flunky, Lefty, and I offloaded the rafts and moved everything away from the muddy streambank. Bogard, Shotgun Eddie, and Cowboy walked to the trail and waited for the water buffalo, then they began loading their gear. Time went fast but we still had a long way to go. McNulty and O'Riley tied down the loads. Everything repacked, we started off cross-country.

The guides didn't know quite where we were but if we kept going south, downhill, we would be all right. Traveling up and over the old logging road, we came to another fork in the road, which actually had a small sign telling us which direction to go. They believed we were within a three- or four-day walk of our truck, which cheered everyone and made us want to push on for the rest of the day.

In an hour we had reached another road. The guides had scouted ahead and returned with the news that a half-dozen elephants with owners were on their way to greet us. With darkness coming, we were invited back to the small logging camp. We were in high hopes of having something else to eat besides monkey meat and rice.

Coming into the camp, we set up and started a fire to dry off our clothes over the flames. The translators with all the tribal people sat around the fire and talked for hours into the evening. The loggers said they had talked to the Chinese soldiers many times. With that we made more plans and called it a day.

At first light the weather was good. We couldn't remember

what day it was; it had been too long. We broke camp early. One of the scouts went ahead and returned with a report. Only a half-day ahead was a good-sized logging camp. He had talked to the loggers along the trail to this camp, which had a very good kitchen. He asked about something to eat. The scouts smiled and said they had pork, sweet potatoes, and homemade wine fermented for the Chinese New Year. It was a tradition. It was served with homemade bread and possibly some chicken; we would all eat good that night.

The Burmese guides knew the logging crews; they were family, possibly cousins or uncles but from a different village. For a small price we could have a good, hot meal, which would be waiting for us when we arrived. They didn't have to say that twice. Everyone nodded their head yes.

Shotgun Eddie and Flunky were talking to Bogard about food and their last good meal. Flunky smiled. "I could eat an elephant."

Bogard replied, "Be careful what you wish for."

Everyone was in good spirits and walking at a good pace. We started to see elephants and loggers coming out from their day's work. All the loggers were three generations. When riding on the elephants, they brought their grandchildren. This had been their way of life for decades.

As we went up a steep hill, we passed by a team of six elephants pulling a twenty-foot log with trainers and children. They all shouted out a greeting of a morning prayer, then our scouts called out their names and their village name. All the young loggers replied with a greeting and their name. Holding onto the elephant's ears, the workers were always excited to see new faces and talk. These men knew everything about the area. Many of the men in the camp were from the Palaung tribe. We talked using our translators as we kept walking along the trail, the teenage Palaung men asking all the questions.

Going up a good-sized hill and keeping to one side of the

~ *MANG YANG PASS* ~

road so the elephant loggers could go about their work, it turned into a long day, along with being very hot and humid. Everyone was happy to take a break under a large teak tree with some of the other younger loggers and their elephants. We had the usual two cans of C-rations for lunch. The scouts had talked with the logging crews, and they told us we would reach a village before dark. This kept everyone moving. The water buffalo were carrying all the heavy equipment but were used to the heat and workload.

Walking along, we talked about the last three weeks and how far we had come and gone. As we came over the top of a hill, we saw the village and young people coming out to greet us. This was our home for the night.

As always we were greeted by the families and offered a bowl of rice. They offloaded our equipment, allowing the water buffalo to move around; they too had had a full day and needed to rest. Tying them up for the night where they could get water and grass to graze on, all animals were treated well.

We sat down around a fire. All the logging crews came in for the evening. They told us about the Chinese soldiers who were in the village five days ago. The Chinese talked quite a while, had a small meal, then were on their way. Everyone was so tired. There was only small talk for an hour or so, then we brought out our hammocks and sleeping bags if they needed them. All were asleep within minutes.

There was no need for an alarm clock; loggers and elephants got up at sunrise. Small groups of young and curious elephants walked around freely, sniffing over the new people and had their trunks going over everything.

They seemed to like McNulty and Shotgun Eddie. The baby elephants were going through their pockets and tried to sit in their laps like puppies seeking companionship. They couldn't get close enough. It was one thing to have a dog licking you; it was another to have an elephant sneeze in your face.

Bogard told McNulty, "If you took a bath every now and then, that may not happen."

One of the interpreters picked up a radio station with some music and a weather report; there would be no rain, and it would be hot all week. Loggers were coming and going. Some teamed up, dragging larger trees out to the road, stockpiling them along the riverbank. It was a community business, and they all shared in the profit. When rainy season came, they would float their trees down to the marketplace.

Flunky told Colonel O'Riley, "Next time you should rent elephants. It would be much faster, and you'd get a ride."

O'Riley replied, "There may not be a next time."

By midday the sun was beating down on us. It was by far the hottest day we had had on this trip. Slowly we came around a small hill that opened up into a very large clearing. The ground was solid stone leading down to a valley. Off to the side we noticed a stream and a large pond. Mothers were splashing and calling their young children. It was a good day to teach swimming. Everyone enjoyed the water. It was obviously a well-used gathering point for the village.

As we walked down to enjoy the neighborhood swimming pool, we noticed a sandy shoreline to one side of the pond, leading down to the clear and cold stream. Here elderly men and women, most likely grandmothers and grandfathers, had buried themselves up to their waist with sand and were holding prayer beads and meditating. They prayed to their ancestors for their family. All the young people were bathing with ten to twelve young elephants and enjoying the sunny day, cooling off in the crystal-clear mountain water. The young folks were using the elephants' head as diving boards.

O'Riley called for a break. We walked over to watch and enjoy all the young kids having fun with their pets. We were told the village was only a short distance away. Everyone knew we were coming and were waiting for the Americans. The village cooks already had a great meal for us and sleeping arrangements. This village was one of the largest. It was another Palaung tribe where the women wore copper bands around their neck. This was a sure sign we were almost back to our trucks.

"I feel like one of the guys in a Lewis and Clark history book," Cowboy said.

Shotgun Eddie smirked and said, "I was waiting for you to say something like that."

We heard a pounding on a steel drum and some shouting. With that the young people started calling to the herd, giving the command for all the elephants to head out of the water and down the trail. As we watched them run for home, we weren't sure who was having the most fun, the small elephants or the children.

Bogard led the team of water buffalo to the village. Children ran along, pointing out their village. The young boys all wanted to walk into the village with us to share the friendly greetings.

Ten minutes away, around a fence into the animals' gate, there was a larger gate for the animals that took us into the first line of wooden houses made up of scrap wood from the sawmill. We walked into the center gathering place. People here lined up, greeting and smiling, holding their hands together as if praying and slowly nodding their heads. This was their way of saying hello.

O'Riley led us through the village. He greeted the chiefs and elders with handshakes and nods. O'Riley put his hands together and nodded his head, the salute to the tribe's people. Lieutenant Anderson walked over to one pack animal and opened up one of the tin boxes to find the field radio. He put a call out. He wanted to hear anything or anybody, but the batteries on the radios were almost dead. He could only pick up a very light signal. We were too far out.

The interpreter went on the radio with his equipment, but

again, no response. The other scout put a call out in Chinese. Wes knew the voice. He replied, saying goodbye and wishing us well, reminding everyone and Colonel O'Riley we were welcome back. The people of China had enjoyed their new friends from the West. Then he sent a reminder to O'Riley and his friends. "Please and thank you for sending out the postcards to my family."

With the batteries drained down, the radio went silent. No more communications.

The scouts knew it was only one day before their home village and their truck. All was going well, and everyone was happy. Calling it a day, we spent the remaining light going over our equipment, trying to lighten our load, if possible. Later we put out our hammocks. All the baby elephants came over with their trainers. They were very curious about the outside world, which they knew little of. Come nighttime the young children lead the small elephants to their holding pen with the rest of the adult elephants.

In the morning, when they opened up the elephants' pen, all the elephants walked over to their mastered home site and waited for the day to start. The tribe people had organized eight elephants to carry us to the next village. They wanted the Americans to know they were always welcome in the villages of Burma. They wanted to make a good impression for our last days and for our travels.

An elephant caravan was in the holiday spirit for family and the young trainers who would be traveling with their own elephants. They loaded supplies in bamboo packs so all Americans could ride elephants and not have to walk. The guides and scouts rode up front with other Palaung tribesmen. We broke camp late, the preparations for travel taking longer. Plus we were tired from the long campaign, but we would move on with some new supplies.

Ten young men with their elephants were in the middle of

the elephant convoy; after they double-checked the gear, they raced off to scout the trail. They all wanted to be the first one back with a report. The Americans and supply animals brought up the rear. The water buffalo were walking freely, enjoying the fresh grass.

As we moved along, the trees and underbrush were so thick there wasn't a way to get off the trail. Some of the young men traveled out ahead of us, scouting and shouting to each other, enjoying their new adventure. Meeting up with another group of loggers, they shouted out a friendly greeting, the new loggers asking a lot of questions. By late afternoon we came over a hill and saw the steep cliffs with the animal pens. It was the village we started out from. We had come full circle.

Chapter 19

*T*eams of four maybe six elephants were hauling teak logs down the center of the path to the river. Some of the trees must have been a couple hundred years old. We got friendly hand waves but kept moving. We had made good time. The crew walked to the all-wheel-drive truck; they were looking for extra batteries in the back storage area. Lieutenant Anderson changed out the old batteries for the new; now we could listen to the radios and use our walkie-talkies. We could possibly be on the road yet tonight.

As the sun reached a high point in the sky, we started feeling the heat. It was becoming another very hot day. All the elephants were instructed by their trainers to cool off and take a long break. Grouped together in the center of a large pond. Again some of Burmese women and men, the elders of the village, sat down along the riverbank and buried themselves up to their waist in hot sand and clutched prayer beads for an afternoon. This saved their energy for later in the day and was the easy way to cool off.

All the Americans moved the camera gear and our other containers of supplies onto the all-wheel-drive, into the cargo bay, sending the adult pack-elephants down to the pond for a well-deserved cooling off. Everyone decided to take a swim and to give up half a day to rest up. It was too hot to do anything else.

McNulty jumped into the driver's seat and discovered that the truck battery had also gone dead. The Palaung tribesmen were talking about pulling it to start. Lieutenant Anderson put out a call in English to anyone who could hear his voice and help. Young Palaung tribesmen were talking about how to prepare the all-wheel-drive, telling us the rear wheels would be pulled to start the motor. They had to send for ropes, which were in the jungle, used for working with the adult elephants.

At first light O'Riley's crew were woken up to see a half dozen bull elephants with trainers. They were talking to their elephants and helping pack up for another day of logging. O'Riley and his radioman, with both interpreters, gathered around the radio calling anyone they could reach, looking for weather information. Flunky and I were talking with the village tribesmen. McNulty was telling them our problem. He liked to talk with his hands and facial expressions. They seemed to understand and wanted to help. In broken English they told us to prop up the rear wheels of the vehicles with logs and make the tires free to move.

Shotgun Eddie and Lefty dug out one side while McNulty and Cowboy dug out the other, leaving the back of the truck supported with logs. Then the tribesmen brought out two large, reinforced ropes and wrapped them around both vehicles' rear wheel. Six adult logging elephants with their harnesses had been waiting and were brought up and commanded into place. Three were attached to each rope. The tribal leader then shouted out and waved his hat in the air. Both ropes tightened up, and the tires were put into motion, the key had been turned on, and the motor was sputtering. All six elephants were at a full run. But with no success. It didn't start.

Without hesitation the tribesmen turned the elephants around and together with the help of the father-and-son teams, they brought the rope back.

The young Burmese men were getting a lesson in roadside automobile hands-on, old-school-fix-it, their father's way. The fathers' showed the younger men where to place the ropes around the tires, and they repeated the process with all six of the elephants lined up. The elderly tribesmen gave a command and again at full speed the elephants pulled the ropes, which turned the tires, which turned the transmission and the motor. Everyone was smiling and enjoying their unbelievable backwoods working skills, like an old lawnmower with a pull cord.

This time the truck started. At first it ran a little rough, but everyone was watching and hoping.

All the tribesmen give a large noisy hoot and holler, like something you would hear at a wedding.

O'Riley told Lieutenant Anderson, "I wouldn't believe that if I hadn't see it. I wish I had the camera or video recorder."

"You do have a camera but it only takes pictures a mile away."

"Get it out. We got time for a picture."

Anderson would have loved to give the tribe some American money, but they didn't know what money was. So he repaid them by leaving almost all our field gear. I offered them two boxes of C-rations. The tribal chief smiled and shook his head no. We couldn't even give C-rations away.

The scouts and interpreters put their hands together, bowed their heads, then waved goodbye.

Cowboy and Shotgun Eddie bartered for handmade tropical shirts, trading for some rain ponchos and army-issue machetes and knifes. They also bartered for handmade crossbows, not to sell or trade but for memories.

With all the tribal people waving and shouting their goodbyes, O'Riley's crew, along with the magnificent seven Army riflemen, had their picture taken with the chief tribesmen and a dozen ladies of the village, who had their tribal copper rings from their shoulders to their ears, and a half-dozen elephants behind them with their young trainers. Off to the side many more of the villagers were watching and enjoying the day.

With a final goodbye, the truck was off. For several hundred

~ MANG YANG PASS ~

yards the village young people rode on their baby elephants behind the vehicle, shouting goodbye.

Driving down the logging road, we were heading forward in time, hundreds of years. It hadn't rained the entire time we were there but the water coming off the mountains and hilltops had caused several washouts. The all-wheel drive could only move along about five miles an hour. We always kept two to four men walking in front of the vehicle, shoveling in washout areas and testing the road. We came to the first village of Bhamo, which had a small garage for vehicles and motor scooters.

Our interpreter went over the battery problem with all six of the mechanics. They appeared to be family and took great pride in their work. They were very skilled for such a small rural town. They tested the battery and gave it an okay. They shut the motor off and started it back up several times. With that we called it a day.

While O'Riley and Anderson were doing all that, we found a bed-and-breakfast for a good place to eat and sleep and possibly a hot bath with soap.

The next day the Burma Road was dry but it was still a slow drive, going through switchbacks and a dozen hairpin turns, all going downhill. A full half-day later we reached Myitkyina airport. Again, four small charter planes, American Airlines Dornier Do 28s, were waiting, compliments of CIA.

The CIA wanted to see the photographs and the film with a full report. Our straggly crew of soldiers had just become a priority.

Loading them up, it was a short hop overland to Manadalay. After touchdown the plane taxied to a large hangar where an American C-130 cargo plane with a full crew waited. They wanted to leave within the hour. We had a dozen ground crew help with loading up the last of the equipment.

We had a very good dinner, complete with knives and forks,

no banana leaves for dishes or fingers for silverware. It was time to sky up with a final goodbye to all the government officials. Next stop, Thailand, then back to the Central Highlands.

Shortly after the plane took off, the pilot told us we were not spending the night in Korat or Takhli. The C130 would be going straight over the border, back into Vietnam and in one day, if we were lucky, we'd be back in our own company.

Later the copilot came back to the cargo bay to tell us the Thailand airport was too busy to bring us in. The air controller told us to go directly to the airport in Long Binh. This was Saigon's airport, which was under the Air Force control.

When the plane arrived, it taxied to an Air Force hangar and was greeted by many Army and Air Force crews and officers. Colonel O'Riley talked with some friends and received orders to stay in Saigon. The orders were handed to him by a group of Army officers. Among them was Captain Shorts himself. He had been ordered out of the country with a promotion and orders to report to the Pentagon. Like it or not, a Washington, DC desk job.

Captain Shorts had been kicked upstairs. Captain Shorts and Colonel O'Riley would travel together to Washington, DC; their overseas time was up. O'Riley gathered all seven of us riflemen together in the storage area to the side of the main hangar doors. We found a place where we could all sit around. Other officers and big brass came over and sat.

O'Riley told me and Cowboy about some deals he had got going on. He wanted someone to take care of the last details with his good friends, the Korean bridge guards. Then he looked at the seven riflemen from the 573 and told us where to find the keys to the warehouse inside our perimeter. It was a very tempting deal and was already set up and waiting for someone.

Lefty, Cowboy, and McNulty were nodding their heads yes. I had been in the warehouse and knew where everything was. I also knew Tony Lee and the other Korean captain; he wanted in too. This was a black-market bonanza. O'Riley talked everything over with Captain Shorts. It was probably the last time he would ever talk to or see any of these soldiers again. The captain told everyone what day and month it was and how long we'd been out. It was easy to lose track of time when you were on a mission. You'd focus on your surroundings and where your next meal was coming from. He told us about what had changed since we had been out.

The entire Wade Davis Marine base was shut down and had all moved out of the Central Highlands. The 573 was on stand-down and in one year everyone stationed there would be going home. Then the captain walked us over to a plywood container saying, "I'm taking Sergeant Schaeffer with me." Then he gave us a smile and told everyone to go ahead and have a look see.

Flunky and Bogard got down on their hands and knees and looked into the wire cage to see a pair of dog ears and a wagging tail. The animal turned around and gave off a bark.

I smiled and said, "They finally have Scheffler in a cage where he belongs."

We all bent over and looked into the kennel. Shotgun Eddie and I started to laugh. McNulty and Lefty bend over and looked into the side window, which was wired over. Tripod was inside and starting to whimper; he wanted out. Stepping to the side, Shotgun Eddie unclipped the door and opened it wide enough for Tripod to come out and stretch his three legs.

Captain Shorts informed us the only way to get Tripod out was with orders and new dog tags. He had made him a human and sent him out as a sergeant. Five-Fingered Scheffler prepared the orders, which he did for a couple of favors.

"I signed and okayed it. Sergeant Tripod is going home with me. I know the rules, but bending the rules for Sergeant Tripod... well, he's worth it. Not for one minute would I think of leaving him behind. And as far as you seven, the 173 Special Forces men and the South Vietnamese, you are all out with the other companies in bullet Hole Woods. You'll be linking up with them in the next few days. I wish I was with you, but my orders are to babysit O'Riley's behind, again. Get him to DC."

With that an Air Force Captain came over and informed us it was time; our plane was waiting. We decided to say our goodbyes under the flagpole a hundred feet away. All seven of us riflemen were going back up to the highlands. We formed an almost-straight line, then gave a casual, sloppy military salute, took one step forward, did an eyes right, and stood at attention.

Captain Shorts, with Sergeant Tripod on his left and Colonel O'Riley and the other staff on his right, saluted back, then we all shook hands. All us magnificent seven riflemen walked over to an Air Force bus, which transported us down the runway to a waiting C-130 cargo plane. The plane taxied to the end of the runway, the pilot received clearance to lift off, and five minutes later we were in the air. Our secret mission into China was over.

CHAPTER 20

The radio tower communicated with the pilot, telling him to stay up over five thousand feet. No dropping down and divebombing their friends by buzzing small airports, something jungle-boy sky-pilots loved to do. But the tower said it wasn't safe today; there were enemy forces close by, ready to shoot down any planes.

It was only a couple hours in the air to reach Pleiku. As we landed, four Army Cobra gunships launched into the air. Shotgun Eddie, McNulty, and Lefty shouted out, "Snakes in the air!" Captain Short's favorite expression. McNulty pulled out his journal and added more notes under today's date. He told us he had enough to write a book.

Flunky and I looked at each other and agreed, we were home now. Ten or more choppers in two columns were in the air going out, moving to our west. The helicopters went overhead. We thought it was the 173 Airborne, possibly being resupplied or going out to bring back returning troops. At the same time coming in were four Huey helicopters with red crosses on their doors, dropping down over at the hospital. One by one shutting down their machines, they began to offload the wounded.

Flunky and I found a vehicle and rode to the 573, driving through Pleiku. As we passed Two Core, we saw the South Vietnamese soldiers had made up a showcase of captured weapons, most of them Russian-made. Five long rolls of weapons from the last six months of pushing into Cambodia. Every time they went over the border, they traveled in faster and deeper into Bullet Hole Woods. The VC and NVA had huge settlements throughout Cambodia. Several hills had been tunneled out and used for storage of military equipment.

Going past the VC prison and Artillery Hill, seven CH 47 Chinooks lifted off and made a straight line going west; all had cargo nets with 105s wrapped up, being airlifted out to a new firebase farther out on a hilltop, all heading for the border. Even though the Army was on standdown and didn't have half the men they had six months ago, we still had to hold our ground.

As we came up to our front gate, six 175 self-propelled howitzers came onto the road, moving at full speed. They came down off Artillery Hill. We followed behind them, all moving through the front gate. They headed for a north side gate and down into the valley. They had been called out as reinforcements.

As we made a turn, we could see a handful of 155 artillery pieces, also moving out at full speed. It was a big call-up. When we reached the CO's office, Sergeant Scheffler and First Sergeant Epler were there. We had no baggage to unload, just what we could carry in our pockets. First Sergeant Epler greeted us with a smile and a salute. Sergeant Scheffler told us the entire company had been out for two weeks and five days. The scouts and artillery spotters had been out three weeks more. That evening or maybe even late that afternoon everyone was coming back, and we would do a full head count.

We all walked over to the mess hall and sat down for a talk. Scheffler told Flunky, Cowboy, and me what he knew. We asked if the CO had heard anything or knew anything about the Navy shore patrol, and if anybody had been killed or medevac'd out. Sergeant Scheffler gave us a few names of those killed, among them Bob Whitelaw. He told us nine guys in all had been airlifted. We lost four others, all newbies, who shouldn't have been out by themselves on point. We hadn't had time to work with them. Newbies died fast. Then Scheffler told us about the company's new mascot as he pointed under the table. Another walking-wounded German shepherd. Some of us bent over and others got down on their knees to see a pair of eyes, his head bandaged up, his two front legs in a cast. He could barely move but his eyes were watching us as if he knew we were talking about him. He was brought in three days ago and was healing up well. They still hadn't found out his name; his trainer was medevac'd out. The cooks called him Grinder; he loved big bones, and he had a very healthy appetite. His right ear had a number tattooed. We would nurse him back to health and hopefully get him home.

Epler told us the last thing Captain Shorts did was to take Billy down to his new home, the Catholic church property, where he was being brought back to his country's traditions. He was teaching English to all the priests and whoever else would sit in. At this point a soldier came in with the news about the troops on the field radio. They were only a half-mile out, coming out of the valley, and everyone was to hold their fire.

With that everyone walked out toward the perimeter. Trucks started to roll out to meet up with the incoming med with ice water. The sergeant of the guard pointed us to the opening in the north wall, which was still open from the artillery pieces that just went out. As we reached the top of the berm, we climbed up onto a truck roof and watched. Several hundred yards out, as far as you could see, the entire road was covered with soldiers marching in. The first line of scouts and Montagnard troops were moving alongside the road. A call came in from the north gate. Their walking wounded were being helped with aid from the other men of their company.

Coming in past the wire and over the berm, the men were offered ice water, the first they had in weeks. Some stopped because they were so overloaded with equipment. Trucks were loaded with broken-down military equipment of all types, moving up the hill to our base camp. Sergeant Sketch was on the perimeter and opened the concertina wire farther; dozens of men were moving in. Within the hour the men on point came out of the valley and up to the fence. Sketch called into the CO's office, telling them to get some food and beer out here. Shotgun Eddie and McNulty were in the CO's office and listening to the calls coming in. It was an old voice they were hearing, a friend's voice. They questioned him.

McNulty gave him a call back. "Is that you, Sketch? Food is on the way."

Sketch asked, "Is that you, Tom McNulty? Where have you boys been? I've got someone's M14, and I'm keeping it. Were you in LBJ's jail again?"

Shotgun Eddie stood in back of McNulty and bent over to reach the microphone. "Who has my hand cannon, you sorry sacks of shit?"

Sketch replied, "All of them are out on supply trucks. We used them on the mission into Bullet Hole Woods.

"We'll all meet up tonight, in the workshop."

I stepped into the office and asked Sketch, "Who's out there with you?"

"Burnie, Breeze, Chico, and Jerry Jeff with Doc Murray and a couple of newbies, who are fast becoming top guns."

I replied, "Bring them to the workshop with you."

Sketch shouted, "Got to be going, business!"

Listening to the microphone, we heard the sound of diesels as they passed by.

Four more self-propelled howitzers and two 155s were moving out and down the dirt road with five men per piece of artillery. All had one or two supply wagons behind them. They would be out for weeks.

Sketch walked around, going back and forth to one of the

gun trucks being kept on the perimeter. Breeze was driving one. Sketch told him who was all back and that we'd be meeting at the workshop later. Breeze was talking with the unit coming up into view, slowly approaching the wire. They wanted the entrance widened. Walking slow with full packs, the 173 was coming in with their company of Montagnard scouts, along with two or three companies of the South Vietnam Army.

Breeze wanted to know about the walking wounded, severely wounded, and did they have any dead personnel? The reply back was no need for medical choppers; everybody and everything had already been airlifted out.

The line of men kept getting longer, moving up into sight. They came out of the valley and began to reassemble. Hundreds of field personnel looked for their people. On their field radios they were in contact with the rearguard, which was spread out over more than two miles. They had been marching the entire day. Two weeks of marching in the bush was showing on these men's faces. You could tell they were tired; you could actually smell their body odors fifty feet away. They were slowly coming in ten to twenty at a time.

The corner towers sent up yellow smoke bombs on their roofs and flares for markers. Coming over the berm and through the wire, they started to form columns and platoons.

The 573 sent out two night patrols with security. The nightly ritual. Other men were helping bring in the last of the soldiers and scouts with all the captured equipment. It took four hours for the entire patrol to come in. The very last were the Montagnards B23 MIKE Force with Special Forces and Green Beret interpreters. Also coming in with the rearguard were some South Vietnamese officers. They were all given good, hot meals, coffee, water, and rice wine. By this time three complete units were now totally inside the wire and regrouping.

Men from the 573 were walking among the troops, making

sure they got a hot meal. Doc Murray and Chico brought out food. Lefty and Ammatwozeo brought out drinks and saluted the soldiers. While the troops were eating, officers from Two Core headquarters and the US Army Brigade headquarters arrived. The Brigade had a small presence in the 573. Two Core and the Brigade walked through the troops, shaking their hands and congratulating them, not only the officers but the field soldiers as well. The soldiers had brought out a large number of weapons and ammunition from their trip into Cambodia. They were all going to march out of here heading for their base camps. It was time to stand tall. They were now all considered to be hard-core field units, experienced full-fledged grunts.

The B23 MIKE Force came together, and we were now actually able to see the entire group. The MIKE Force had the best scouts in the entire area. They always split up and were sent off in many different directions to help the other troops. Their knowledge of the Central Highlands was immeasurable.

After eating and resting, everyone formed into three columns. All the soldiers were in good spirits and joking about their next trip out. Loosely formed squads and platoons were shouting and smiling.

The scouts and rearguard of the B23 MIKE Force were resting and eating and talking with the men of Special Forces. They were congratulating each other. With the help of the Montagnard's MIKE Force, they were able to push much farther across the border into Cambodia, which had been the Montagnard's hunting grounds for years. They still had many miles to walk back to their villages.

The Montagnards soldiers had kept many of their wounded with them; they took care of their own, but Doc Murray was considered to be one of them; they trusted him with their lives. He was cleaning up the wounded and sending several to the field hospital. It was then Doc Murray heard his name called out.

~ MANG YANG PASS ~

Looking around he saw someone he knew only too well, a field commander and son of the village chief. It was Lieutenant H'Yua Liana. Doc had patched H'Yua Liana up months ago.

They did their best to look like soldiers but they were not soldiers; they were scouts. More than a dozen of them carried handmade wooden cross poles with arrowheads dipped in urine and excretions. Montagnards troops knew a lot about scouting but very little about marching in straight lines. Several trucks arrived with the wounded and equipment. Doc Murray and the Special Forces personnel were gathering last-minute essentials for the field hospital and their three-day stay, where they would see dozens of Montagnards people of all ages. Some GIs wanted to help and chose to spend the night in the Montagnard villages. In the morning they would patrol out with Special Forces. Many more volunteers than were needed wanted to go out to the village to help for security.

This village was more than nine miles out on a mud road. Half a dozen trucks were rolling up to load up for the trip out. Many of the Americans were close to these primitive people. Having spent entire weekends in their village, several men had actually deserted the Army and moved out to one of the villages and had gone native. The Montagnard people were not part of Vietnam's government so they had no rights or say in their own country. They lived in a part of the world no one went to. All the villages look to be hundreds of years old.

While this was going on, all the other troops were forming up to march. They were trying to remember how to march. They unfurled the South Vietnamese flag, the American flag, and the South Korean flag. Some fifty men from the White Horse Korean Calvary would be in the front and lead off the march. This had been their position in the field the entire time. The Montagnard troops had no flag; they were not considered to be Vietnamese, so they would march with the Special Forces and the American flag, only until they reached the front gate, at which point they would disassemble. They would have to march past Brigade headquarters, then the 573 headquarters. Sergeants were shouting, "Straighten out," "Clean up the uniforms!" The soldiers sent all the heavy equipment to the rear and placed everything on four-wheeled, off-road vehicles called mules. They had eight or ten of them bringing up the rear.

The field units were ready and were given the order to start their march. It was ten hundred yards to the front gate. The captains and lieutenants of the South Vietnamese Army shouted, "Okay, you heard the order to march!"

Two long columns moved forward, singing behind their flags. The 173 stood and formed into squadrons, then platoons and prepared to march. Platoon sergeants came alongside and called out a rhythm. "Your right, your left, your right, your left." Then the platoon sergeants started singing with the men.

"Your mother was home when your left, your right, your sister was home when your left, your right, sound off, one, two, three, four. Raise your head, hang it high. The 173 is coming by, your right, your left.

"Send all my belongings to the next of kin; chances are you won't see me again. Pack my bags, bury my bones, the 173 won't be home. Your mother was home when you left, your right, your sister was home when you left, your right."

The platoon sergeants yelled to the men, who were still carrying eighty pounds of field gear and captured weapons, to do their best to straighten that line. The men in their platoons, some who hadn't eaten a sit-down meal or any meal in the past three weeks, were calling each other every name they could think of, trying to impress the big brass. With red faces and clenched fists, they shouted out, "You Girl Scouts get to sleep in a bed tonight!"

The GIs looked at each other and smiled. This was the life of the ground pounder. They made it out alive. Their singing was terrible, and their marching was even worse. As they passed through the front gate, they had gone full circle, all on foot. Tired and dirty, if they were told to do an about-face and go back out, every last dog soldier would not hesitate.

After the Montagnard troops walked past Brigade headquarters and were saluted by all the officers, they marched to the front gate and were told to wait for a ride. The convoy of trucks rolled past the security fence of wood and into camp where the Montagnard soldiers were given a hero's welcome by their families. The soldiers were all proud and happy to be back. Young men and women were building up the fires, as they always did when some of the men spent the day away. They had caught fish in the river and lake that were next to the village. Other groups were going out on a hunt and others, mainly the elders with the children, had been doing fieldwork the entire day in the rice paddies. For this night, the ladies of the village had prepared a large meal for all the returning soldiers.

Rice bread and many of the fine foods, pork or duck, was cooked up in a stainless-steel pot, which was a souvenir to them some time ago. They only ate raw meat in the morning. The Montagnard all loved raw fish. While fishing, the Montagnard people swallowed fish whole, the same as a bird would do. Headfirst. One swallow. It was high in protein. This evening the entire village celebrated the return of their soldiers, who were also the village's security force and always carried weapons with them. The Americans brought out some special foods and two bottles of brandy, and a long line of clay pots full of Montagnard moonshine made for a great supper for their friends and family in the village.

The 173 moved past Artillery Hill on the left and the tank

farm on the right. Just half a mile down the road, with the order "Column left" and with pride and their heads up, the 173 marched into their compound. The 173 was told by the United States Army it was put on stand-down notice. The 173 gave Washington notice back; they would not stand down. The 173 was the first in and would be the last unit out.

∞

Still marching for another half mile, the South Vietnamese reached Two Core. They were all ready for a rest, wearing three weeks of dirt and sweat from the bush. Carrying full packs, the line of men was almost a half mile long.

∞

Back at the 573, evening formation started. First Sergeant Epler called out names.

"Cowboy, Shotgun Eddie, Flunky, Scheffler, JV, and McNulty," and ten other names, "report to my office after formation."

When we arrived in the office, Epler and the new captain, Captain Brown, were standing together. Epler gave us the news. "You have two or three days to collect your 201 files, turn in your equipment, and pack up for home." Then First Sergeant introduced the new captain, who gave us a small speech about our sloppy uniforms, telling us the 573 would be standing down in the next six months to one year. Brown complained about discipline. "I can't get half the men to salute me." He also complained about the lack of soldiers; he couldn't do his job with the number of men he had. He was going to make the men of the 573 stateside-quality soldiers.

Hearing that, I made a sound like a duck quacking, voicing

my disagreement the only way I could. Flunky gave a turkey call. We were in the back of the group and couldn't be seen.

"I'm going to clean up this unit and make these men military soldiers again.

"Norman Shorts told me you men were a bunch of undisciplined, trigger-happy loose cannons and a bunch of kleptomaniacs. He called you a very well-organized group of horse thieves and cattle rustlers, but you couldn't steal horses or cattle for the simple reason there were none to be found. And I see what he means. Half the trucks in our motor pool belong to the Navy and Air Force."

Captain Shorts had always turned his head and looked away. He could frequently be heard saying, "I don't want to know."

Somebody in the 573 had tried to steal an elephant but couldn't get it onto a truck. After a half day of phone calls, they took it back to the village, claiming they found it walking around. Captain Shorts found out about it from a radio call he received from the commander of the Air Force flight control, telling him the 573 should keep their money; they didn't airlift large elephants.

Captain Brown turned around and gave everybody a hard look, telling the soldiers in front of him, "I called the Air Force commander, who told me he talked to the leader of this scrounge team. The commander had a conversation with a man who calls himself Five Fingers."

At this point Scheffler got up and walked out of the room. Walking past his friends, he ran his fingers across to his mouth horizontally as if to say, put a zipper on your lips.

"Captain Shorts has been promoted and sent to Washington to the war department. The US Army and the government has ordered him back to be an advisor to the entire US Army and all the other armed forces. He came into country as a captain but has been promoted to a field commander. He will be missed. Our duties now are to deal with standdown and defense. A second wall of defense inside the outside perimeter is going to be constructed. We're going to lose control of the Central Highlands if we don't step up the bombing.

"Many men will be going home in the next few months. All you here have orders for home, but I would like to ask if anyone would like to reenlist and stay on with the 573 for the good of your country. You have a day to think about it or to finish up all your businesses, say your goodbyes, and collect all your paperwork for your 201 file. The hospital has your medical records that are not at the Air Force Base, and all the other paperwork is at the colonel's front office." With that he told us we were dismissed, and we walked out of his office.

We headed for the motor pool and found the field radio to make a call out to the Montagnard village, hoping to communicate with Doc Murray. For the last six months Doc had been operating his own hospital for all the Montagnard villages. He talked to several other doctors and nurses to come out for half days and help with surgery and, if necessary, bring the severely wounded out by truck to the Red Cross Center, the hospital in Pleiku. At first they were a small volunteer medical center in the Central Highlands village, but as the word got out, more people started showing up. Wounded and ill Montagnard soldiers brought in their families to help feed and care for them. The American medical teams did their best to beg, borrow, and mainly steal medical supplies that were needed. It was not enough, but everything helped, and we hoped for the best.

CHAPTER 21

Coming out of the mahogany forest, following the river leading up to the village, we begin seeing familiar faces.

Doc Murray and his medical crew looked over the last of the young men. Some of them were yet to become teenagers. They knew in the morning there would be more people at their door, people needing medical attention. No one was turned away. Doc Murray had been known to help a water buffalo with an infected eye. He and the other volunteers also did medical training for the village people. Hopefully, this would help keep them well after the Americans had left. Overall, they were very healthy. The medical crew did everything they could. Sometimes it included taking off their T-shirt and using it for a bandage. With limited resources and usually no hot water, once a week, if possible, the medical team wanted to see anyone with a problem. If they were bad enough to need an operation, they brought them back to the Pleiku hospital.

൸

At the 573 they were putting together the list for the night's security on the perimeter. First Sergeant Epler walked around, calling out names of men who he had orders for, walking through the mess hall then back into the CO's office. He handed the

~ JAMES VOELKER ~

paperwork to Sergeant Schaeffer. "You probably know where they are."

Gary Schaeffer took the orders and immediately radioed Doc Murray, looking for us. "Field hospital calling out the good news; everyone's orders are in." Schaeffer waved his own orders in the air, shouting out, "I getta go home too! I've got walking papers!"

Doc Murray took the call. When he heard the names being read off, he replied, "Yes, they're out here." Then he walked out to the fire pit to tell us to saddle up. He called out, "McNulty, Flunky, Shotgun Eddie, Cowboy, Lefty, Bogard, Smoking Joe, and JV, you got your walking papers. You're going home."

We wanted to head back to camp in the morning. It was late afternoon, almost dark. Cowboy and I got back on the field radio and talked to Scheffler. "We can't get back before noon, if that. Hold the orders."

As the day ended, Doc Murray saw his last patient and he closed up his small hospital for the night, then walked over to the fire pit. He had a great meal while sitting around the fire. Doc Murray put more wood on and talked with the children from the village, who always followed him around. The team of medics were enjoying the fire, watching the small children playing, coming and going in groups. They talked about the future of the village and its people. The war had brought the Montagnard people into the world of today and they were not ready for it.

As always we bedded down for the night around the fire pit and watched the last of the flames in the clear night sky. With a cold wind coming down from the north, we tipped our heads back and watched the evening stars coming out. It was our last night in the high country.

In the early morning, three men were chosen to be on point for the walk back to the 573rd. Bogard, Smoking Joe, and Lefty were the first ones up and agreed to move out. Packing up their gear, they had a last look around, then found their way through the barricade of ten-foot logs and branches and through the front gate. They turned around to look back.

Many of the villagers had walked out with them and were standing in a line. In their uniforms of handmade clothing, steel pot helmets, and flak jackets that were way too big for them, they waved their weapons in the air. The men of the 573rd did the same, without telling them we were leaving them and not coming back. The villagers' only replacements in this war were their own children.

For a second time the three Americans turned and raised their guns up, and the Montagnards troops waved back. This village with rusted tin roofs and dirt paths surrounded by rice paddies hadn't changed in many lifetimes.

McNulty, Flunky, Cowboy, Shotgun Eddie, and I said our goodbyes to Doc Murray and a handful of his volunteers, who were going to stay behind for another day or two. Walking back through the hospital, we passed young men who had lost an arm or a leg and villagers who agreed to serve with us even though they only had bows and arrows and handmade spears; their numbers were dropping fast.

We slowly packed up and looked at the faces of all the families we had been sharing time together with. We threw our gear on and walked away, following a muddy path, down and out of the mountains and over a dike between two fields of rice that followed along the hill and disappeared on the backside, where the forest took over.

Our path continued to another larger rice paddy, where the barefoot farmers were beginning their day planting. We moved right along; we wanted to beat the afternoon heat. It didn't take long to catch up with the men on point. We talked about the end of what we had started to become. We had turned from soldiers to cowboys, our own vigilantes.

Together we walked down the path to the last Montagnards campsite, where we took a break. We were out of the last of the foothills. We took it all in, knowing this was the last time we would see these third-world people, who were now inviting us to join them at their campsite to enjoy our last sit-down with the tribes' people.

Having breakfast around the open fire, we had a meal of watercress and rice. Then with a goodbye, and the last look at the civilization hundreds of years in the past, we finished our trek back to the 573.

I got on the field radio to the hospital in Pleiku, calling for

~ *MANG YANG PASS* ~

someone in record-keeping, asking for our medical papers to be pulled out. The radioman in the hospital called back within five minutes. He told us our papers had already been pulled and picked up by the company clerk two hours ago. "The clerk has a company Jeep and is with three other soldiers. He told us to tell you to meet up at the shortcut."

With that done we all agreed to a last visit to our favorite brothel, a goodbye to the girlfriends and a last shot of Saigon tea. We hitched a ride. Going through downtown Pleiku, we told the driver to drop us off at the new church to say goodbye to Billy. We all wanted to know if we could do anything to help his living conditions and possibly get an address to write to him.

Chapter 22

The church compound was a busy place with many people walking around. We received a friendly greeting, and we asked if we could see our friend. One of the young priests took us inside. We found Billy giving an English class to his new family of Catholic priests.

Billy said excitedly, "Everyone, there's going to be a wedding, and we were just in time to become witnesses! Tue and Steamer will be here within minutes; good timing. The wedding will begin outside the chapel."

This marriage gave Tue more rights from her country to become an American, a citizen, a "war bride." Legally married and recognized by the government, it was a great moment. Steamer and Tue were starting a new life. They were waiting for his friends and her family to make plans for the event. Tue and the lady family members arrived in two Lambretas. They were all dressed in white silk Vietnamese-style dresses. A half dozen men on small motorcycles also arrived for the wedding and were greeted by the priest and Billy. Everyone was very happy to be involved in the wedding. Several of the men had been working on the new church. Billy was happy to see all these familiar faces again. Tue, with her family and friends, came over and talked with Billy.

Tues told him, "I'm so very happy that the priest and church agreed to everything on such a short notice."

Tue introduced her two sisters and two brothers, then several of the priests told us it was time to begin the wedding. We were all led to a corner of the courtyard under the shade of a large tree, where it was cooler and relaxing. All were seated to watch. There were not more than a dozen people and the priest kept it short.

Everyone was very happy and ready to give out congratulations. Billy wanted to talk more with his American friends about his life. He had questions about what was going to happen to him but no answers from the Catholic priest, who didn't know about the American stand-down orders, big questions about what's going on in the countryside with so many American units leaving.

One priest wanted to show us their newest building, only five hundred yards away. It was made by hand. All the stones were brought in from the countryside, and the concrete was made inside the building. All the material was being brought up with wheelbarrows.

Billy said he had also been working with the masons, learning new skills and making new friends. He wanted to know if we could sneak him a base field radio – a Squawk box – with batteries. Billy said it would help everybody. We agreed to get it for him to keep in contact with all the other troops and friends, but he had to hide it somewhere. While teaching his fellow workers English, he was starting a new life, but it was slow. Billy had heard about the standdown while living with his people, and he realized what was coming. He was strong-willed and kept his head up, still hoping for paperwork for an adoption. First Sergeant Epler was still in charge and had four months' time to work on his adoption paperwork.

The priest told Billy, "In the morning you are going to have some visitors, officers from Two Core." These soldiers were Billy's commanders. They were young officers and would be starting to visit him once a week and talk with him about his new duties to his country. He would be learning the South Vietnamese military rules and be brought in as a young field grade soldier, involved with intelligence and communications.

I took one last photograph of him.

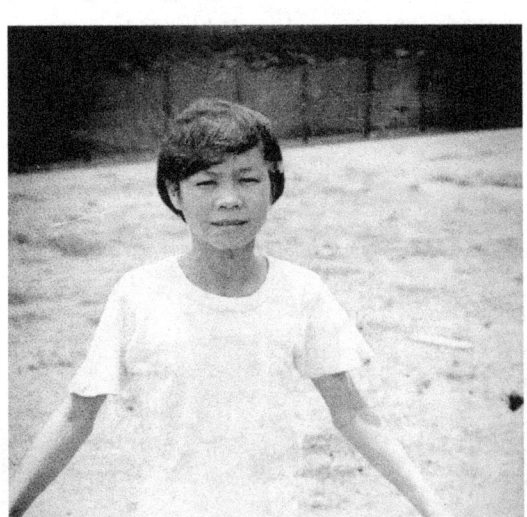

When it was time to leave, I asked the priest, "Could I bring down a mattress with sheets and pillows for Billy?"

The priest replied, "Billy must learn to sleep the same way all priests do, on a bamboo mat."

He was not going to get any special attention; he was now a Vietnamese.

After the wedding ceremony, two priests talked with

Steamer and his new wife. They needed a signature from the two of them and the families. The wedding certificate was proof for the Vietnamese government offices in Saigon. They were told by one of the priests that they may still have to pay off a government official someplace along the line. This would help Tue for her trip back to the states as a war bride.

With the paperwork all taken care of, Tue and her sister, Suzanne, would be going back to their house for a celebration with family and friends. Everyone was invited but the head priest would not allow Billy to go to a brothel.

We walked across the courtyard, over to the main gate to the road. Billy and I stood together. I got down on one knee so we could look at one another. I can still see his face yet today. Back then he was only four feet tall and seventy pounds. Flagging down a truck, we said our last goodbyes. While he stood and watched us disappear, the image of him and the feeling of him being my younger brother had disappeared over the years. He was too young to be a soldier, but he had to do what his country was requesting.

Hopefully, someone would be able to come back and bring him out. He and his country were heading into a very hard life.

Bogard and Shotgun Eddie were shouting for me; they wanted me to hear the news. The truck driver from our company told us there was a big deal going on at Two Core. We had extra time so we went. We all wanted to see what was going on; even the driver wanted to look at all the captured weapons. Many South Vietnamese soldiers were busy on the front lawn of Two Core. Pulling over with all the other vehicles, we couldn't believe what a huge stockpile of weapons they had collected. Taking a few photographs while walking through the lines of weapons, some of which we recognized from all the trips into Bullet Hole Woods.

The lines of a cache of r75 mm recoilless weapons were on display.

~ JAMES VOELKER ~

It was a combination of Chinese, Russian, French, and recaptured American weapons, many mortars, most of them from World War II. Some were weapons that our company had personally brought out some months ago. Other weapons came in over the years from many sweeps over the border. Walking to the back left corner, we found a half-dozen Russian 51-caliber machine guns on wheels. Those were our favorite weapons for spare parts and reconstruction for our hand cannons. Even though all of us were leaving in forty-eight hours, we still wanted to walk away with several of these magnificent machine guns.

We asked about buying them, but no one could give us an answer. Then we were told nothing was for sale. We all talked it over and looked at all the fences and security and we realized we didn't have time; we had to give up our old ways of doing business in the Army. Then we got the great idea to head to the shortcut for the last hug and kiss goodbye.

As usual the shortcut was very busy in both directions. Shotgun Eddie, Bogard, and I jumped off at Tue's crib. Coming inside we found Breeze, Cowboy, Flunky, and Lefty all enjoying some Saigon Tea. Later, Scheffler joined us. He was just two buildings down, saying goodbye and received a Vietnamese back walk from

~ MANG YANG PASS ~

Suzanne. We all went out to the courtyard and spent the afternoon under the banana trees, next to the pond. We hung out with small children who spoke fairly good English even though they were not even five years old. They were running around doing table service, wanting to be helpful, enjoying the company.

The pond was very peaceful; families of ducks wandered through, going from one neighbor's pond in the community to the next. As the afternoon celebration began, many of Tue's friends and family arrived with specially prepared meals just for the day. A card game got started with all those willing to join in. Eight men on a ground-level table were playing poker and betting with miscellaneous Vietnamese and American paper money and some small gold bars. Tue's two brothers and her friends were enjoying the day of card games.

Tue's younger brother, Mue, knew his way around a deck of cards. He also worked in his father's motorcycle shop. Mue talked a lot, had secondhand knowledge about the US Army and was always friendly, asking questions about the Army. Mue was sometimes a little too curious and you had to watch what you told him. Like most Vietnamese men, they had to play both sides, friendly to us and the Viet Cong.

After an hour or more, they called for some uncooked duck eggs for a side snack. Tue brought over two dozen and gave them to Mue. Duck eggs were high-energy but didn't have much taste. They were a specialty when you were drinking in the middle of the day, and we were all given one. Mue told us how to eat them. He put his head back, cracked the egg open with his teeth and dropped the egg into his mouth, then swallowed. Thinking it was just an egg, Scheffler, half-drunk, with Flunky and me, followed Mue's instructions. Then we realized to our surprise what we had swallowed. We had just eaten an unborn duckling, feathers and all.

This ended the card game. We found Steamer and Tue and

gave all their friends and family a last handshake. They showed us the paperwork all signed and the sealed wedding document. They requested a photograph of the two of them together with Tue's father.

Scheffler reached into his backpack and pulled out our medical and dental records with everyone's 201s. He had added other paperwork, which was personally put together in the CO's office. He had been busy repairing all the paperwork to cover our behind, our behavior. Back in the states we would have been given dishonorable discharges. In Nam our shenanigans gave us a "higher rank," literally and figuratively, which would give us more privileges. I was also given the rank of E4, which opened more jobs and better jobs, and could actually give orders if I wanted to. The Army knew the outpost forts were only held together by teenagers.

Scheffler told Steamer about some downtown government people he knew for under-the-table paperwork for his new bride and would have to talk with Brigade headquarters about trying to get Tue out of the country. Brigade controlled all the units in our area. But he couldn't guarantee anything.

Steamer had to follow up on all the paperwork and make friends with the new captain; no more stealing his Jeep and driving it down here. If he wanted to get anything done, he had to be prepared to pay off the government officials in Pleiku. The wedding certificate and the Vietnamese Catholic priest would help her.

We gave a final goodbye to all our girlfriends, and minutes later we flagged down a truck that was heading for the 573.

In the evening formation we were handed our walking papers and told if anyone had a sniper rifle, we needed to hand it over to someone with all our field gear. Captain Brown also wanted to know about Sergeant O'Riley's warehouses.

There were ten of us that had our orders, but in the past month we had only received two replacements. We had five more, but they reenlisted, signed up for two more years to get out of here and sent to Germany. In the last thirty days the 573 had dropped down to less than one hundred men – a skeleton crew.

After the formation was dismissed, Lefty, Cowboy, Chico, Smoking Joe, and Doc Murray stood around talking shop. Scheffler and Burnie were talking to the captain, then Steamer came over and talked about the wedding. He showed the captain the certificate with the signatures and dates from the priest and explained who the best man and witness for the ceremony were. Billy wanted to know if we could help him get out of the country. Captain Shorts and Epler were willing to meet them within the next few days. Shotgun Eddie and Scheffler told the first sergeants that Billy had been promised a field radio. "Can you sneak him one?" It was the best way to keep in touch with him.

Off to the side of the group, Jerry Jeff was getting all choked up and had a lump in his throat. He was being left behind; he would have to find somebody new to run off the road. I took some last photographs and gave my best wishes to Steamer, who was still talking with Scheffler about one last big favor before he left. Breeze came over with Yogi. I asked for Yogi's real name and his home address so I could write to him. After knowing him for ten months, I was just now finding out his real name. A couple of the new guys walked over in field gear. They were just getting ready to go out to one of the listening posts. It was night duty two or three miles out on the perimeter with only one experienced soldier in a group of ten.

Everyone started giving the newbies advice about staying quiet and moving around two or three times a night. Breeze talked with Flunky, who was showing him how to adjust the M14 scope for accuracy for longer shots and told him where to find all the parts he needed to build his own hand cannon in the dugout. They all started talking about who was driving the old gun trucks and who was going to be the new radio person, talking over all the bad turns on the roads to the coast. Flunky and Breeze gave each another a biker's handshake: the two distrustful soldiers. Together they leaned forward and locked arms at the elbows and agreed to do a road trip. Flunky said, "Remember Las Vegas." Breeze agreed and added, "Remember New Orleans for Mardi Gras. Bring Bogard too, if he's not wanted for anything in any of those states!"

With the goodbyes behind us, we couldn't help feeling that we were letting the company down by leaving. Burnie from the Whiskey Train, with Yogi from Big Daddy Virgo Rat, came over and requested everyone's home addresses after we got resettled. We all walked over to the motor pool where they were making preparations for the next run, which was going to be in three days. We had thoughts about leaving but even more thoughts about what was going to happen in the Central Highlands. Almost half the fire bases along the border had been abandoned; Artillery Hill didn't have the personnel to put out to fire bases anymore.

We all spent the rest of the day in the motor pool, helping friends. The conversation turned to what exactly was in Sergeant O'Riley's warehouse. We all agreed to send a truck over and clean the place out before someone else did; it was our last night. We turned the keys to O'Riley's warehouse over and they agreed to send out a search team after dark.

We spent what was left of the day checking over the trucks for the next convoy, as if it was normal. Then we walked over to Alice's Restaurant, the armory. It was the last night, and we spent time with the new personnel, training in the gunsmith shop, rebuilding weapons, putting parts together, making hand cannons. We were giving them their first lessons, hands-on, working under kerosene lanterns and candles. The new soldiers were being shown how to keep all other weapons clean and running. We assembled their ammo belts to be ready to go out on short notice. A wooden table had gun parts from twenty or more 50 calibers. All the men were sitting on benches on both sides of the table, showing the new personnel how it was done and talking shop. At the far end of the reassembled table were three finished products, which were ready to be zeroed in.

All new soldiers were also given a long list of places where to borrow equipment for resupplying fast. Everyone was ready. We disassembled our hand cannons, taking them outside, setting them up on sandbags. All three hand cannons were loaded with tracers. The new men were positioned behind their new weapons to get the feel of a single-shot M2, Ma Deuce, their very own hand cannon. When they were ready, Lefty gave the signal to Cowboy, who called out to the perimeter and Sergeant Sketch. Cowboy told Sketch it was nighttime target practice, so three guard towers sent up a flare. Sketch replied when Cowboy called back, "Send it now!"

With that, three flares were in the air from three different guard towers. Lefty told the new snipers to take a shot, then added, "Remember, always lead a moving target twice the length of movement. As the tracers go out, they can mark your targets and accuracy."

Sergeant Sketch sent up flares from different towers six more times, then called it a night. With kerosene lanterns and guns in hand, we went back inside for a last class of basic M2, 50-caliber training. They adjusted their telescopes for windshear and distance. One of the new snipers believed the best way was to have a second person as a spotter. The experienced snipers nodded their heads and agreed. We decided we needed to eat so we left everything on the workbenches.

Men were coming in the dugout with trays of food from

the mess hall, sitting down and enjoying a cold of beer with supper and the company of soldiers. Most of them would sleep in hammocks for a couple of hours before going out on guard duty. It was the last night for us so we couldn't help but think about our last duties for the company. Everyone went their separate way, some of us going back to our hooch for the last time. They took anything worthwhile to the laundry and supply room to turn in our gear. Some guys wrapped an old towel around their neck and put their soap and shaving equipment into one pocket. That's all they had to take with them.

Some men had a camera but not much more than that. The old backpack and smelly sleeping bag with the mosquito nets were left on our bunk. Maybe someone could use them. We decided to spend our last night in our hammocks in the cargo bay of our gun trucks. We had already signed out of the company and didn't have to make morning formation. We were no longer part of the 573.

CHAPTER 23

On the last morning all the men leaving ate together. Walking out of the mess hall, we could hear a vehicle coming out of the motor pool. We turned to look down the road; it was one of the gun trucks. We couldn't see the vehicle's name, but its smokestacks had flames coming out; they had already added the JP4. Chico was in the cargo bay. They were coming in too fast, and it was getting louder.

Almost hitting another vehicle, they drove alongside the boardwalk as smelly green wastewater splashed the boardwalk and everything else. We knew it had to be Breeze in Instant Hell. He cranked the steering wheel and downshifted, bringing the truck in sideways, up against the boardwalk. Bogard, Scheffler, and I joined McNulty in the cargo bay. Then Flunky, Shotgun Eddie, and Cowboy threw their gear in and climbed in. We added more JP4 jet fuel and left for the Pleiku airport. Breeze was learning fast; he was going to be one of the worst drivers in no time.

On the way McNulty and Shotgun Eddie talked about what great pizza they were going to have, one of the first things they did when they hit their hometown. McNulty told Bogard and Lefty about Chicago-style pizza with double toppings eaten at the concert in the park at the Chicago waterfront.

Then with a big smile, he revealed a small secret. He was leaving the country with some military hardware. He stood up and lifted up his pant legs. Laced into each one of his boots was a military 45 revolver, which was now stolen property. When we questioned him about it, he told us, "I'm going to be somebody when I get home to the south side of Chicago."

When we reached the airport, we were told a C130 would be leaving for Da Nang in one hour, our freedom bird back to the states. The plane had room for twenty more men. We all smiled and grabbed hold of our small backpacks.

Other companies were gathering together for the plane ride. We could hear Artillery Hill working out, sending rounds to the far corners around the airport. They did this to protect the aircraft. The C130 taxied out and warmed up at the end of the runway. A Cobra helicopter came alongside and escorted us off. It was a short hop into Tuy Hóa where they offloaded supplies and material and a dozen men returning to their units.

Landing in Da Nang, the largest airport in the country, nonmilitary commercial planes were waiting. An Air Force bus took us to a residence's departure area where we handed in our paperwork, our first stop before we were brought to the assembly area. We were given a barracks for twenty-four hours, while we waited to fly out. Sitting around waiting to hear about our flight times, 201 files in hand, Sergeant Scheffler talked about the last two days of paperwork he filed in the 573 company office. He wanted to leave the Army in good shape. But before he could finish, everyone saw a buck sergeant walking over. He looked like he was on a mission. We all watched this stateside wannabe, who was now running.

McNulty said loud enough for everyone to hear, "Look, it's a stateside super trooper! It's captain ugly-do-right, and he's coming our way."

I laughed and said, "I need some lipstick. We're probably going to be kissing his butt to get out of here."

~ MANG YANG PASS ~

Our tin-soldier sergeant started shouting orders and running off at the mouth.

"Tell everyone I am in charge here. Fall in! Departing this area, your orders go through me. Is that clear?

"You all look like dirty animals. You are no longer in the Central Highlands, and you will not be wearing those uniforms out of here. We don't want you getting these privately owned aircraft filthy. I want to see all you grunts in new uniforms, right now! March down to the Army supply and draw out all new uniforms with your rank and name tag and hats. And for those of you who forgot and don't wear T-shirts and underwear, draw those out too. You're not leaving looking like field units!"

The sergeant in charge had his uniform ironed and starched with creases in his pants, something you don't see in the highlands, not even with officers. He stopped in front of Flunky and eyed him up. Flunky didn't have on any headgear. Instead, he had taken two cloth sandbags, cut the top off and made them into a stocking cap to keep his balding head warm and protect it while wearing his steel pot. The sergeant liked his little kingdom where he could play God over field units, telling us he was going to keep our orders, even if he made us wait three or four days. Then he started in on Flunky's sloppy uniform. McNulty and I just laughed.

Funky eyeballed up his new little friend, then moved one step closer to him and threw him a kiss. In a friendly, low, calm voice he told the little Hitler sergeant, "I'm going to turn you into a Girl Scout. I'm going to cut your marble bag off."

His right hand wrapped around the handle of a fourteen-inch Montagnard knife that he always carried. He called it his good luck piece. His left hand reached for the Boy Scout standing in front of him, calling him dirty names.

I held down Flunky's hand. Scheffler stopped him from moving forward. Scheffer called the 573 squad to attention and to fall in. We did an about-face and moved off as ordered. Scheffler looked over at his squad and, shaking his head, asked if we remembered how to march. We did our best and with a little help got pointed in the right direction. We had become a little lax in discipline.

First stop was the barracks. Scheffler told everyone, "I've got a surprise. I've typed up military paperwork and orders to get us out of here, no sweat.

"It's also a good time to look over your medical file and remove any documents you don't want to go home with. I've gotten mail from men who just went home warning me about stuff in their 201 file. The VA has rules about our conduct – your article 15s need to go.

"I've got the current situation under control. That little pantywaist Nazi is in for a little surprise."

Scheffler handed everyone the medical form with their name on and told us, "You all have a history of lower spine and neck injuries, up to 20 percent disability. It needs special medicine and a medical examination." Then he said we could and should remove any medical papers that say we were hit or wounded by friendly fire.

Shotgun Eddie and Cowboy looked at him and asked, "What are you talking about?"

Scheffler smiled. "You know what I mean, when you got those penicillin shots for the clap."

We all immediately went through our medical paperwork. Shotgun Eddie and McNulty threw out a couple papers. I removed one page. Cowboy and Shotgun Eddie discussed which month we were on R and R in Bangkok. We all looked at Scheffler and realized how devious this guy was.

I asked, "How did you get to be an E6 sergeant and get away with all this?"

Scheffler replied with a big smile shaking his head, "I'll give you one guess. It's *Lieutenant* Scheffler, and I have top-level government security. I put in paperwork three months ago and gave my rank and position to tripod."

Most of these guys had known each other for ten months; in Vietnam that was half a lifetime. Cowboy, with a strange look on his face, took his paperwork to Lieutenant Scheffler. He gave him a big smile and asked, "Well, Mr. Natural, how did you ever get a degree from the University of Indiana? Tripod could type and spell better than you and he's only got one front leg."

Garry Scheffler went through the papers he brought from the CO's office. He smiled and said, "I gave myself orders months ago, but don't tell Uncle Sam."

Bogard was laughing with the rest of us. He lifted up one of the papers from his file and shook it at Scheffler. "Just so you know, in the states THE is not spelled T H A."

Scheffler replied, "It was an old typewriter. I got through the University of Indiana by working in record-keeping at the Dean's office and paid my way the same way. I sold a couple dozen degrees every year; had to have the paperwork backdated and in order."

Scheffler smiled and handed out other paperwork. "Stating now all you are E6 sergeants, except for McNulty, he's a first lieutenant."

After looking over all the paperwork, we headed back down to the supply building to draw our new uniforms with our names and new rank. We casually formed up and marched back to the assembly point. We hadn't been this clean in months. We smelled and looked as if were just coming in, not going out. We fell in line with four other groups of men departing. We had been field units so long we had forgotten all the basics of the military and could have cared less. The sergeant in charge was treating everybody as if they were stateside. He had nothing better to do than play soldier. When he finally got back to our squad, he noticed right off we all outranked him. Suddenly, he took a different attitude; the little Nazi sergeant didn't want to deal with us. He could play the cat-and-mouse game with the other soldiers.

He informed us we were not spending the night. There was a plane yet today we could make. Looking over the group of men, he had to keep a civil tongue in his mouth. We were given back our 201 files and orders and told to hurry. He saluted us and called out, "Dismissed!"

It was only a five-minute ride out to the plane. While they offloaded from the last military ride, we mixed in with civilians and government contractors. The airport looked more like someplace back home. Everyone was wearing clean clothes, carrying briefcases and suitcases, no weapons of any kind.

It was over. It felt like we had been released from prison, convicted of false charges. My thoughts turned to what was going to happen to the men of the 573. There was not much left of our company. Half the buildings on the base were empty; the central highland was going to go back under the control of the North Vietnamese military.

Going back to the states was now starting to feel like coming out of the old Southwest. We were a bunch of cowboys and horse thieves, guns for hire, soldiers of fortune. We were going to have to change our ways. We were now coming forward one hundred years into civilization. No more outdoor toilets, no brothels, no longer washing up with your helmet. We wouldn't be sleeping on the ground, waking up soaking wet from the rain. No more Madame Butterflies and Saigon Tea. We had to get real girlfriends and real jobs. Forget about everything. Maybe or probably start thinking about some good lies and or keeping our mouths closed about some duties we had to do in this country.

Most of us were twenty years old, maybe twenty-one. Like most men in our company, we had blood on our hands, most of it the enemies, some of it from doing one of our own who deserved it. It was good to forget all the faces and to start remembering our own families and going by our real name. We needed to figure out what we wanted to do with our lives. I didn't want to be night security guard for some warehouse. Back home my high school classmates were in their second year of college and many who stayed home were still bragging about their athletic ability. Not us vets. The Pentagon called us "throw-away soldiers." We were about to get the best runaround of our military career.

The jet plane's door opened up, and we walked up the stairs.

McNulty looked around but stayed with the group and kept to himself. There was nobody searching us or our belongings, so he got away clean with his 45s.

Stepping onto the plane, I didn't bother turning around. Everyone was talking about the states and more than happy to be seated. I had one last look out the window. This was where the story ended.

∾

To all my veteran friends from the 573 after fifty years of life, I took time to write this in hopes someday maybe we will have a reunion. Sink, I'll remember you forever. I'm two days older than you, but you're gone. I miss you, man. Don't know where your gravesite is, but I intend to find it. I had all your personable items: your pictures, your collection of Montagnard knives, and one of your dog tags with several other dog tags from our departed friends. From our nights of sitting around the fire pits on Saturday evening or Sunday morning, and again talking to one another in the gun box, we all made the pledge and promised. We knew some of us weren't going to make it and that someone from their gun crews would personally deliver a dog tag to their family's front door. I had your mother's address in Connecticut. I'm going to see her after I get out of the VA hospital; I don't have a car so

~ JAMES VOELKER ~

I will hitchhike. (I was told to report to an Army hospital when I reached Fort Lewis Washington and start treatment for malaria. Without knowing it I had lost a third of my body weight.)

    I had four more family's addresses, one in the Southwest and the others out on the west coast. I'll send off a letter first. I know Jim Kelly's family lives in Portland Oregon. I will not take off my dog tags before I see my duty done. We will talk again. I know you're still up there running the Pass. Doing the road with all the other drivers, radio men, gunners, and second gunners. When it's my time and I lay it down, I'll put my flak jacket and steel pot back on and join you. Just so you know, Sink, I killed the man who killed you. When we took you out of the gun box of Ground Pounder and walked you over to the third helicopter, we left your eyes open so you could watch. After our silent minute and heads down with a last goodbye, Captain Shorts closed your eyes and then closed the helicopter door. Four days later I earned my tattoo; my right arm was given the same tattoo as yours, an A+.

    Billy, this book is for you. I hope you're still alive.

    To this day we are all reminded of that country on the other side of the world. After fifty-plus years, Billy is still talking to us. Maybe we will meet him in the afterlife, in the fields of ambrosia. Only visions of faces, nightmares, and sleepless nights follow us, but we had our orders.

    If the United States Army calls me up again, I will go.

ACKNOWLEDGMENT

First and foremost I need to thank my daughter, Angela. Without her help and constant support, this book would never have seen the light of day.

I would also like to thank Christine Keleny of CKBooks Publishing for all her help in editing and publishing, and Dana Zwaska for her wonderful job proofing.

About the Author

James Voelker is a Vietnam Veteran who volunteered to serve in Vietnam in 1969. His training was at Fort Campbell, Kentucky. As soon as he got there, he was told, 'listen up, take orders, and sign up for extra training.' His unit was the last unit to be trained on the M-14 rifle.

Upon arriving home in the United States, Jim spent a year running dog tags to various families of men in his unit. Then he spent a few years in Colorado exploring.

Today his career as a carpenter is still somewhat active. In his free time he enjoys working on his house, watching old movies, writing, and spending time with his grandkids.

If you enjoyed this book and think it's important to support our veterans, please leave a review online. Jim would greatly appreciate it.

I came into the 573 the end of August. My birthday was two weeks later. I was nineteen going on twenty.

Everyday life in the 573 was a little of everything: you helped the company maintain control of the Central Highland by going on patrol; you might have night guard duty on the camp perimeter; or you could be a crewman in the gun box in a resupply convoy. "Doing the road" was a job. The convoy consisted of about eighty men, and guard duty was for everybody. The first sergeant would come looking for you with work assignments, and you wanted to be on his right side.

Crewmen also worked on their trucks or their guns. The motor pool had a junk yard for parts. And we had no water in camp and had to drive to a lake five miles away, two or three times a day.

Standdown started in 1971 March. The 573 went from 300 to 250. When I went back to the states in September, the 573 had only eighty to ninety men left. I moved around for three to four years looking up men's families.

~ Jim Voelker

Made in the USA
Monee, IL
13 January 2024

50554275R00129